Trouble on His Wings

SELECTED FICTION WORKS BY
L. RON HUBBARD

FANTASY
The Case of the Friendly Corpse

Death's Deputy

Fear

The Ghoul

The Indigestible Triton

Slaves of Sleep & The Masters of Sleep

Typewriter in the Sky

The Ultimate Adventure

SCIENCE FICTION
Battlefield Earth

The Conquest of Space

The End Is Not Yet

Final Blackout

The Kilkenny Cats

The Kingslayer

The Mission Earth Dekalogy*

Ole Doc Methuselah

To the Stars

ADVENTURE
The Hell Job series

WESTERN
Buckskin Brigades

Empty Saddles

Guns of Mark Jardine

Hot Lead Payoff

A full list of L. Ron Hubbard's
novellas and short stories is provided at the back.

*Dekalogy—a group of ten volumes

L. RON HUBBARD

Trouble on His Wings

Published by
Galaxy Press, LLC
7051 Hollywood Boulevard, Suite 200
Hollywood, CA 90028

Printed in the United States of America.

ISBN-10 1-59212-336-8
ISBN-13 978-1-59212-336-0

Library of Congress Control Number: 2007903534

Contents

Stories from Pulp Fiction's Golden Age

A ND it *was* a golden age.

The 1930s and 1940s were a vibrant, seminal time for a gigantic audience of eager readers, probably the largest per capita audience of readers in American history. The magazine racks were chock-full of publications with ragged trims, garish cover art, cheap brown pulp paper, low cover prices—and the most excitement you could hold in your hands.

"Pulp" magazines, named for their rough-cut, pulpwood paper, were a vehicle for more amazing tales than Scheherazade could have told in a million and one nights. Set apart from higher-class "slick" magazines, printed on fancy glossy paper with quality artwork and superior production values, the pulps were for the "rest of us," adventure story after adventure story for people who liked to *read.* Pulp fiction authors were no-holds-barred entertainers—real storytellers. They were more interested in a thrilling plot twist, a horrific villain or a white-knuckle adventure than they were in lavish prose or convoluted metaphors.

The sheer volume of tales released during this wondrous golden age remains unmatched in any other period of literary history—hundreds of thousands of published stories in over nine hundred different magazines. Some titles lasted only an issue or two; many magazines succumbed to paper shortages during World War II, while others endured for decades yet. Pulp fiction remains as a treasure trove of stories you can read, stories you can love, stories you can remember. The stories were driven by plot and character, with grand heroes, terrible villains, beautiful damsels (often in distress), diabolical plots, amazing places, breathless romances. The readers wanted to be taken beyond the mundane, to live adventures far removed from their ordinary lives—and the pulps rarely failed to deliver.

In that regard, pulp fiction stands in the tradition of all memorable literature. For as history has shown, good stories are much more than fancy prose. William Shakespeare, Charles Dickens, Jules Verne, Alexandre Dumas—many of the greatest literary figures wrote their fiction for the readers, not simply literary colleagues and academic admirers. And writers for pulp magazines were no exception. These publications reached an audience that dwarfed the circulations of today's short story magazines. Issues of the pulps were scooped up and read by over thirty million avid readers each month.

Because pulp fiction writers were often paid no more than a cent a word, they had to become prolific or starve. They also had to write aggressively. As Richard Kyle, publisher and editor of *Argosy*, the first and most long-lived of the pulps, so pointedly explained: "The pulp magazine writers, the best of them, worked for markets that did not write for critics or attempt to satisfy timid advertisers. Not having to answer to anyone other than their readers, they wrote about human beings on the edges of the unknown, in those new lands the future would explore. They wrote for what we would become, not for what we had already been."

Some of the more lasting names that graced the pulps include H. P. Lovecraft, Edgar Rice Burroughs, Robert E. Howard, Max Brand, Louis L'Amour, Elmore Leonard, Dashiell Hammett, Raymond Chandler, Erle Stanley Gardner, John D. MacDonald, Ray Bradbury, Isaac Asimov, Robert Heinlein—and, of course, L. Ron Hubbard.

In a word, he was among the most prolific and popular writers of the era. He was also the most enduring—hence this series—and certainly among the most legendary. It all began only months after he first tried his hand at fiction, with L. Ron Hubbard tales appearing in *Thrilling Adventures, Argosy, Five-Novels Monthly, Detective Fiction Weekly, Top-Notch, Texas Ranger, War Birds, Western Stories,* even *Romantic Range.* He could write on any subject, in any genre, from jungle explorers to deep-sea divers, from G-men and gangsters, cowboys and flying aces to mountain climbers, hard-boiled detectives and spies. But he really began to shine when he turned his talent to science fiction and fantasy of which he authored nearly fifty novels or novelettes to forever change the shape of those genres.

Following in the tradition of such famed authors as Herman Melville, Mark Twain, Jack London and Ernest Hemingway, Ron Hubbard actually lived adventures that his own characters would have admired—as an ethnologist among primitive tribes, as prospector and engineer in hostile climes, as a captain of vessels on four oceans. He even wrote a series of articles for *Argosy*, called "Hell Job," in which he lived and told of the most dangerous professions a man could put his hand to.

Finally, and just for good measure, he was also an accomplished photographer, artist, filmmaker, musician and educator. But he was first and foremost a *writer*, and that's the L. Ron Hubbard we come to know through the pages of this volume.

This library of Stories from the Golden Age presents the best of L. Ron Hubbard's fiction from the heyday of storytelling, the Golden Age of the pulp magazines. In these eighty volumes, readers are treated to a full banquet of 153 stories, a kaleidoscope of tales representing every imaginable genre: science fiction, fantasy, western, mystery, thriller, horror, even romance—action of all kinds and in all places.

Because the pulps themselves were printed on such inexpensive paper with high acid content, issues were not meant to endure. As the years go by, the original issues of every pulp from *Argosy* through *Zeppelin Stories* continue crumbling into brittle, brown dust. This library preserves the L. Ron Hubbard tales from that era, presented with a distinctive look that brings back the nostalgic flavor of those times.

L. Ron Hubbard's Stories from the Golden Age has something for every taste, every reader. These tales will return you to a time when fiction was good clean entertainment and the most fun a kid could have on a rainy afternoon or the best thing an adult could enjoy after a long day at work.

Pick up a volume, and remember what reading is supposed to be all about. Remember curling up with a *great story.*

—Kevin J. Anderson

KEVIN J. ANDERSON *is the author of more than ninety critically acclaimed works of speculative fiction, including* The Saga of Seven Suns, *the continuation of the* Dune Chronicles *with Brian Herbert, and his* New York Times *bestselling novelization of L. Ron Hubbard's* Ai! Pedrito!

Trouble on His Wings

Chapter One

JOHNNY BRICE lounged in the shade of the hangar, eyes half-shut, cigarette smoldering, forgotten in his fingers, thinking about absolutely nothing. He should have known better. Every time he had ever relaxed in his life, Fate had sent her legions scurrying and foraging for some trouble to get Johnny into; and this time was no exception.

Running footsteps turned the end of the hangar and Johnny, with a chill of premonition, glanced up to see Irish Donnegan, his pint-size coat holder and mechanic, come tearing up in a cloud of dust and sweat. Johnny deplored such activity on a warm day.

"Johnny!" cried Irish. "Look, Johnny! Gee gosh—!"

"Hold the pose," said Johnny with a sigh.

Irish panted, swallowed and then, eyes starting from their sockets at the effort, slowed his speech. "Johnny, the *Kalolo* burned this morning at sea! Twenty lives lost! Ship abandoned, passengers and crew taken off by the SS *Birmingham Alabama*. Thrilling sea rescue, women and children—drama!"

"You got to quit this excitement," sighed Johnny. "It'll get your cerebellum displaced and your liver cirrhosified!"

"The old man is wild. He found out some of the passengers had hand movie cameras and he bought all the film aboard

3

by radio. He's getting out a special release and he needs that film in three hours, and the rescue craft is still two hundred miles at sea. He says you gotta get an idea. He says you gotta get that film. And you know Felznick!"

Johnny took one last drag of his cigarette and threw the butt away. "An' he said that I could have a month off for gettin' those hurricane pictures. Irish, take my advice. Don't never get efficient in the newsreel business. Here I am, my bruises hardly healed and my pay unspent and we gotta go chasing after some film two hundred miles at sea. Am I a cameraman or an errand boy? Is this a job or a hard way to commit suicide?"

"We ain't got much time," panted Irish. "Gee, think of it, Johnny. The *Kalolo*, biggest round-the-world ship, burning to the waterline, boilers exploding, women screaming, men gettin' burned alive! Gosh, Johnny, I bet if we'd been there we coulda made an epic, huh? I bet we coulda got some swell shots."

"Yeah," said Johnny. "You sure can think of some of the damndest things."

"You got an idea yet? Old Felznick is on fire. Never heard him so excited. He said get right out there and check the rescued list."

Johnny

4

Irish

"Huh," said Johnny with a start. "Wasn't his wife comin' back from Europe on that tub? What a guy! His wife may be burned up—and he thinks of special editions. Come on, fellah, I think maybe I've got us an idea, at that."

They headed around the corner and zigzagged their way through the hangar to the amphibian. It was one of three company ships, squat and sleek and powerful, its wheels sticking out of the big fuselage like short lizard's legs. On its side was the red-and-gold insignia of the outfit, a lens emblazoned with the words, "World News, 'The Best First.'"

Johnny signed to a mechanic, who swiftly dollied the ship out on the tarmac with a small electric tractor. Irish eagerly slid into the rear cockpit and threw the starter switches. The big engine clanked and wheezed, and then with an angry roar blasted a dust-filled slipstream back into the hangar.

Meantime, Johnny was struggling into a parachute. When he had fastened the webbing about his legs and shoulders, he dragged a small hand camera out of the locker and draped it around his neck by a strap. Stuffing a rubber film protector into his overalls, he started toward the amphib.

His way was blocked by a man built of spheres, a man who looked like anything but the ace cameraman of "Mammoth Pictures, 'All the News Always.'"

"Goin' places?" said Bert Goddard innocently.

Johnny slowed down with great unconcern. "Hello, fellah. Say, I got a hot tip. There's a big oil fire over in Jersey. Million-dollar blaze. Got to cover it right off. Ain't you heard about it?"

Goddard grinned complacently. "You know, Johnny, little boys that tell lies never go to heaven. It's something in the shipping lanes, says that amphib."

"Why, Bert, you never heard me tell a lie in my life. Honest, it's just an old old fire—"

"Goddard!" bellowed a teletype man from a nearby office. "The *Kalolo* burned at sea!"

"My pal," said Goddard.

"Well, I tried anyhow," said Johnny. "Besides, we bought all the amateur film aboard not half an hour ago."

"How you goin' to pick it up?"

"Guess," said Johnny, adjusting his harness and surging past.

"Y'damned fool," said Goddard. "Y'want to get yourself drowned?"

"I regret that I have only one life to give to my company," said Johnny above the clatter and clank of the engine, as he climbed in.

"I'm going to get some air shots, anyhow," said Goddard.

"Take your pick," said Johnny, grasping the controls.

He let off the brakes and the amphib wallowed ahead, wings flashing in the Long Island sunlight. He kicked her around into the wind and lanced down the concrete track and into the air.

Irish pulled his hood shut and clamped the radiophones to

his ears, listening attentively. Finally he tapped Johnny on the shoulder. "Course ninety-three degrees, there's a thirty-mile tailwind at two thousand."

"Gotcha," said Johnny, banking into the course.

Far behind them, the smoky towers of Manhattan gradually sank down under the horizon. Below and ahead, a steel-plated sea with a crisscross pattern of waves, small and distinct from this height, tried to appear innocent after a roaring night of it.

Calmly Johnny scrutinized each ship in the lanes below, checking off freighters and tugs, as he tried to locate the SS *Birmingham Alabama*. At long last he saw a pillar of greasy smoke on the far horizon and knew that the rescue ship must be almost directly below. Then he saw it, a child's toy on a mirror. He shook the stick and Irish took over.

"Here's the automatic," said Johnny, handing back the small camera. "After you drop me, take a turn around the *Kalolo* out there and get some air shots of it. Then come back and put her close to the rescue ship. When you see me dive overboard, put her down and by God, I'll break your neck if you make me swim more than a hundred yards."

"You goin' to jump?" said the startled Irish, getting white and tongue-tied.

"Sure."

"But . . . but gee whiz, Johnny, maybe the chute'll sink you. I thought we'd land and let that rescue ship pick you off—"

"That captain wouldn't stop for us," shouted Johnny above the engine's drone. "He'll have to pick me up if I'm in the water. It's my only chance of getting aboard. They'll send out a boat—I hope."

Irish was speechless, forgetting that he had the stick in his hands until the amphib started to come up into a stall. He leveled out hurriedly and, with fascination, watched Johnny stuff a checkbook into the rubber container and then push back the hood to stand up into the blast of air.

Johnny, taking cautious holds, worked his way out on the wing, a hundred-and-eighty-mile-an-hour wind making his overalls thunder against him. He glanced back at Irish, who nodded. Johnny tightened up on his nerve. He always hated a jump, hated the wind in his nose, blowing upward until it felt like he'd lose the top of his head. Sea and sky were too much of a shade to be detailed. He hurtled down through a blue void, only occasionally catching sight of the rescue ship below. He felt for his heart to see if it was still beating, that being the best method of locating a rip cord, never held at the beginning of a drop, lest it pull and foul on the ship.

The smooth sensation against the seat of his pants told him that the chute was pleasantly sliding forth. For a moment of chill he wondered who had packed it, whether it would crack open. Water split a free-falling body into chunks. Abruptly mighty hands grabbed him and tried to tear him apart, and then swung him in a long, dizzy arc, with the great white umbrella tipping slowly high above. He caught his breath, cursing the wind in his nose.

"Hell of a life," Johnny told a sea gull.

He slipped the chute, to get more directly in the path of the SS *Birmingham Alabama*, which now began to have planks in its deck, and lettering on its lifeboats and a cloud of smoke pluming back from it. People were staring up at him in wonder.

*He hurtled down through a blue void, only occasionally
catching sight of the rescue ship below.*

Johnny put his hands on his harness buckles so he could dive out before the chute collapsed over him. The sea, which had looked so smooth, was now a series of mountain ridges and green valleys.

"Hope it isn't cold," shuddered Johnny.

It was. He went into the depths, to be jerked back to the surface like a torpedo. His chute was towing him, and he fought for the release of his buckles. Before he had them, the silk was soggy and collapsing. As soon as he was free he worked to keep on the surface, wondering urgently if the SS *Birmingham Alabama* still had a few sea traditions kicking about in an old locker after one big rescue the night before. Would they put out a boat?

Tossed to the crest and let down like a roller coaster into the trough, he could not see what was happening, save for the growing bulk of the steamer. Was it going to run him down? For the matchstick thing it had appeared from the air, it certainly was increased in size. Johnny hadn't ever seen anything so big.

He was growing tired, and the chill was eating through him like knives. Wouldn't the fools ever get busy? Were they going to let a guy drown?

Suddenly a boat hook fixed on his collar, choking him. He was towed to the gunwale of the lifeboat and sailors snatched him over the edge, to drop him in the bottom, like a floundering cod.

"Okay," said the mate, standing at the tiller. "Prepare to give way. Give way all together! Stroke!"

Johnny sighed with relief and watched the brawny sailors

heave-ho on their oars, sending the lifeboat on its crazy, tipsy journey back to the side of the drifting steamer. Johnny grinned a little to himself. It wasn't everybody that could stop a ship like that.

Tackles were hooked into the boat fore and aft, and blocks creaked as they were lifted up the palisade of rusty steel toward the boat deck. The davits swung, first one, then the other, and the lifeboat was over the side and back into its cradle.

A thunderously scowling man wearing tarnished braid, fastened upon Johnny. "What's the idea? I thought your ship was coming down, but it's flown off by itself! Is this some new kind of a ———, ———, ———, ——— stunt?"

"Johnny Brice, of World News. Get your picture in all the theaters, Captain—"

"News! Why, you young—"

"Ah, ah!" warned Johnny. "Ladies present, Captain." And he slid out of the irate mariner's grasp and through the crowd.

As he went, a young lady suddenly backed out of the crowd and appeared to be on her way into a passage. The movement attracted Johnny's eye and the girl looked as though she was unhappy to be noticed. Johnny decided that it might be shock from the wreck. She was too beautiful to be swimming around in the ocean and scorched by flame.

"World News," said Johnny. "We bought some pictures by radio. Whoever's got 'em, trot 'em out." He spoke to the crowd but he noted that the girl was more uneasy than before, though reluctant to retreat. Her wide blue eyes were almost frightened, strange in their intensity upon him.

Several passengers ran to get their salvaged films. There

were plenty of rolls, thanks to the penchant of tourists for movie cameras.

"Sight unseen," said Johnny. "Five hundred dollars a roll."

A little fat man wearing nothing much more than a blanket, but gripping his precious film, stared at Johnny with disbelief. "You won't even have to see if it shows in the pictures?"

"Somebody was bound to get some," said Johnny. "Come on, the rest of you. Shell out." He took his checkbook in hand and started to write.

Ten minutes later he had spent three thousand dollars of company money and had a questionable batch of film rolled up in his rubber bag.

"You're a fool," snapped the captain, still peeved. "You could have bought all this when we docked. You won't get it there any sooner."

"Oh, won't I?" grinned Johnny. "Collect from the company for the delay. World News pays for its exclusives."

The amphib was hovering in the sky and Johnny turned to the passengers. Again he noticed that the girl shrank back, though her appearance and not her conduct made the bigger impression upon him. In this mob of out-of-shape men and variously misbuilt tourist women, all in blankets or borrowed sailor clothes, the girl was the only one whose poise was not shattered by exterior appearance.

Johnny moved over to the rail, taking the captain with him. "Have you got a Mrs. Felznick aboard? A sort of lumpy old dame, I think. She'd have her hands full of jewels if she drowned, unless she let go."

The captain had melted ever so little under the persuasive smile of the young man. It was said in the business, that Johnny could talk and grin his way through the place to which all newsreel cameramen probably go. Calling an officer of the ill-fated *Kalolo,* the captain put the question.

The man, singed and chagrined at the loss of his ship, shook his head impatiently. "Just finished compiling the list. We haven't any such name aboard this ship—and we haven't our passenger list, though there's a duplicate in the company office. I seem to remember the name, but—" he swallowed hard. The loss of passengers was too heavy upon him, "But I guess she must have been among the dead."

"The old man is going to take this hard," muttered Johnny. "Thanks, Skipper, for the lift."

"Huh?" said the captain.

Johnny had acted before anyone else realized what he was doing. He went over the rail in a long, clean dive, far out from the ship, so as to miss the propellers—if he could. He came up and saw the side terrifyingly close to him. He struck out as fast as he could, rubber container clutched against his side. The steamer swirled on past to leave Johnny floundering and half-drowned in the boiling wake. He fought to keep afloat, spluttering and coughing. The world was a tangle of green mountains, snowcapped with froth, and all the peaks were falling in upon him. He turned about wildly to locate Irish and found that he faced the stern of the slowing steamer. And as he looked he saw a white figure perch on the rail and soar seaward, straight into the propeller boil. He had no time to speculate on the identity of the mad diver, he was too occupied with the possibility that he would be keeping company, in a moment, with a chewed-up corpse.

"And me without a camera!" he swore.

The steamer had stopped its way for a moment, but now, with a sizzling sea curse the captain rang for headway and the SS *Birmingham Alabama* departed from Johnny's life, just as abruptly as all things parted from a man in such an unstable career.

He heard an engine barking and bellowing as a cunning hand worked the throttle to keep the nose into the waves. A wing was a few feet from Johnny and he thankfully struggled toward it. As it dipped, he grasped it to be pulled bodily out of the sea with the ship's next lurch. Ducked twice, he finally made the catwalk to find Irish wildly pointing to starboard.

"What's the matter?" shouted Johnny. And then he needed no answer. Somebody was swimming strongly toward them and Johnny understood that the propellers had been cheated of a meal.

He edged out on the wing and extended a hand, and then, from wonderment, almost withdrew it.

"What the hell are you doing out here?" snapped Johnny.

The girl he had so favorably noticed was too exhausted to speak as he hauled her up on the wing. Irish was wailing from the pit, madly jockeying stick and throttle to keep the overweighted wing up, crying to them to come inboard, before they all drowned. The ship was going like a bucking bronco, and each smash of the waves seemed hard enough to be the last.

Johnny gripped the leading edge and worked himself along, pulling the girl by the arm. Presently she was helping him as much as she could, and they came to the cockpit, dizzy with so much erratic motion, blind with spray and half strangled by the blast of the slipstream. Johnny boosted her into his cockpit and climbed in with her, slamming the hood down before they shipped any more sea.

"Take off!" he bawled to Irish.

The amphib floundered, plowing water as it strove to get up speed. Gradually Irish, by a process of hauling back and easing off on the stick, got the plane to traveling crest to crest. At last, with a smoothness which was pure pleasure by contrast, the amphib was in the air, picking up speed.

The SS *Birmingham Alabama* went under their wings, the captain shaking his fist from the bridge. But neither Johnny nor Irish even bothered to look.

The girl was shivering and Johnny gulped with embarrassment. In all the commotion he had not realized the scantiness of her costume. She had had but a few ounces of clothing left when she had cast aside her blanket. The shipwreck had found her in bed and only her silk lounging pajamas had been salvaged. But sea water does not tend to improve the modesty possibilities of silk. Johnny pulled a leather jacket out of the locker behind his head and draped it around her. Then he pulled a thermos of coffee and a cheese sandwich from the seat locker under him. She gave him a grateful glance with those blue eyes of hers which warmed Johnny far more than the coffee he poured for her.

They were too tired to raise their voices to the volume necessary for speech behind that yowling engine, but speech didn't seem very necessary at the moment. They sat munching the cheese sandwich, each with half, and sipping the coffee, gingerly held so that the air bumps would not slop it, and were grateful. There is a welding quality to great danger mutually experienced.

Irish, popeyed from the inner pressure of the questions he ached to ask, razzed the engine unmercifully on the homeward journey. Johnny glanced at the watch and noted without surprise that they had been gone two hours and five minutes from Long Island and there was the East River, swarming with traffic, under them. Irish was volplaning down to a landing, picking his way through the puffy tugs and importantly waddling ferry boats. Skirting the stern of a disdainful steamer, he let the amphib settle. She had no more than touched when he gunned her toward a ramp.

A moment later the wheels were down and bumping against underwater concrete and Johnny threw back the hood, standing up. "Here's where we stop," said Johnny.

She clutched his hand in terror. "No! NO! Don't make me get out! Please don't make me! You didn't save my life just to make me lose it!"

Johnny looked at her in wonder.

"Why did you think I took such an awful chance?" she wept.

"Publicity," said Johnny. "It's all right. We'll fake—"

"NO! Please! No! No publicity. Don't mention that you saw me. I don't think anybody saw me dive from the stern of the steamer. That's why I risked the propellers and swam underwater most of the way to your plane. Don't let them get me, please, please, please!"

Perhaps it was the tone of her voice. Perhaps it was because she was beautiful even to beauty-surfeited Johnny. Perhaps his thirst for mystery, news and trouble caused him to act as he did.

"If that's the way of it," said Johnny, "it's okay by me. Hell, I mean . . . shucks, I wouldn't turn you over to anybody."

"Don't say you've even seen me," she begged, her small mouth quivering as though she was about to cry.

Seeing that what she had been through had brought her close to hysteria, Johnny was swift to acquiesce. Holding his rubber container, he stepped down to the wing.

"Irish, you've got to take off right now for Long Island. Make sure nobody sees this girl. I'll be back as soon as I deliver these."

"Who is she?" cried Irish eagerly. "What's her name? What'd she almost bump herself off for? How come she don't want nobody to see her—"

"Take an order without questions, for a change," said Johnny.

"Okay," said Irish, after making the effort and winning.

The girl had dropped out of sight in the cockpit, but now she called to him again. "If you value your life, you won't mention my presence with you to anyone. They . . . they'd get you too, for helping me."

"Not to a soul," said Johnny, hurrying away.

"Gee," said Irish as he turned and started for his takeoff.

Johnny, water still running from him, got behind the wheel of a car parked in a garage near the ramp. Careening it out into the street he started full-speed uptown. A traffic cop saw him at the next corner, started to stop him, recognized him and abruptly headed his machine in the same direction, opening his siren wide to clear Johnny's way for him.

A few minutes later, Johnny skidded his car to a stop before the World News building and leaped out.

"Thanks!" he yelled to the cop.

"Don't mention it, Johnny!"

Johnny scorned the elevator and thundered up to the third floor, bursting into the office of Frank Felznick. He presented the container with a swoop that flirted water over the desk.

Felznick, a tall bundle of nerves with deep, electric eyes, pushed all his buttons at once and grabbed the container, opening it to pour out the eight- and sixteen-millimeter rolls. All his doors opened at once and he threw the precious film into outstretched hands. The doors slammed and a newsreel was on its way to the making.

"You got any word of Louise?" said Felznick quickly.

Johnny hesitated, and then shook his head. "You sure she was on the *Kalolo*?"

"I don't know. I told her to take it. God, Johnny, you understand that? If she's dead, I'm the one that's responsible. I chose the boat." He rummaged in a cluttery desk drawer and finally hauled out a crumpled and unframed photograph, staring hopelessly at it.

"Maybe she didn't take it," said Johnny helpfully.

"It would be the first request of mine she ever obeyed," said Felznick. "She was over there spending all her money on phony titles and I said Paris was no good for her. I talked to her on the phone. Half an hour I argued with her. I told her to take the *Kalolo*."

"Did she say she would?"

"She . . . yes, she said she would. But to think, Johnny, if she's dead, my last word to her was spoken in anger!" He moped over the picture.

Knowing the suddenness of Felznick's moods, Johnny waited patiently. He doubted that Louise Felznick had taken the *Kalolo*, knowing of her activities as slightly as he did, through the pages of society magazines. Felznick had hair-trigger emotions and would never pass up the slightest chance to be dramatic about his affairs—after he had taken care of business. Johnny got a glimpse of the picture. It showed a tall, languorously beautiful woman posed with a baby.

"I didn't know you had a kid," said Johnny in astonishment.

Felznick looked annoyed. "That's Louise's by her first husband. Name's Jack. I—" and Johnny recognized by his tone of voice that here was another act, "I haven't got an heir of my own, Johnny. I haven't got anybody to leave this mammoth business to."

"What's the matter with Jack?"

"Too young to think about. Not mine. Johnny, when I think of how I've worked and slaved to build up this business, only to put it into the hands of strangers—"

"Wait'll you get old before you worry about that," said Johnny.

"I'm forty-eight," said Felznick, looking sad. Another thought struck him and he brightened tremendously. He grabbed his phone and bellowed for the press relations department. "Boys, get a release out on Mrs. Felznick. I'm broken-hearted, get it? She's supposed to be on the *Kalolo* and listed with the missing. Paint it up big. Dig out some swell pictures. 'Movie Magnate's Family Feared Dead!' And lay heavy on that 'Felznick, brilliant owner of World News.' Okay." He hung up and realized that he looked too pleased. "Don't think bad about that, Johnny boy. It's even possible that she *was* on the *Kalolo* so I ain't lying too much."

Johnny was seasoned to press stunts, but he was slightly annoyed that he'd be caught in this one. "You mean there wasn't any chance she was on it?"

"Hardly any. I booked the passage so her name's on the passenger list. I'll let it ride two-three days unless the boys in France find she's still there and ballyhoo it. Boy, that's publicity, Johnny. I need some good publicity. And say," he cried, jumping up, "you're soaking wet. Here, have a drink. . . . Have another drink. That's right." He yelled into his interoffice phone, "Call my car for Mr. Brice. Okay, Johnny, that was a swell job. By the way, how did you do it? You'll get a bonus for this, have anything in the shop. Vacation, anything."

Johnny took the drinks. He needed them. Presently the car was announced and he started to the door, with Felznick pumping his hand and telling him what an asset he was to the company.

"Anything in the shop, Johnny. Just ask for it. I—"

"Mr. Felznick," said a dried-up little gnome whose rubber apron smelled of bromine.

"Wait a minute. And Johnny, I can't tell you how much I owe you. This scoop is perfect. In the New York theatres tonight, before the news is twenty-four hours old. That's the way to—"

"Mr. Felznick," said the gnome urgently.

"What?" said Felznick, annoyed.

"Them pictures you sent in. Every roll's been spoiled by sea water."

"What?"

"And the hand camera roll was a blank," added the gnome apologetically.

Felznick assumed a calm mien. He was never dramatic when he was really mad. "How much did those films cost?"

"Three thousand dollars," gulped Johnny, dismayed at the treachery of the passengers. Too late he recalled that the rescue ship had pulled almost all of them from the water. Why hadn't he inspected the condition of the films? And what had Irish done with that hand camera? It was supposed to show the wreck itself. He was numb with the shock of the first bad play he had pulled in years. And now Bert Goddard of Mammoth Pictures would have a scoop for himself!

"Oh, lord," groaned Felznick. "Deliver me from fools. Grant! Davis! Thompson! Stephens! Kennedy! Meet the SS *Birmingham Alabama* at quarantine; you get a plane and get some shots of the floating wreck; you get some pictures of some families. Kids crying for daddy, and all that. Come on, let's go!"

"What about me?" said Johnny cautiously.

"You?" said Felznick. "You? Go over to Long Island, Mr. Johnny Brice. Just as soon as I get an assignment that's an 'assignment,' you'll know what about you."

Johnny sighed dolefully, battered by the hurrying crews who raced past him and down the stairs. "Seven years in the racket and that's the first bull." He shook his head and moved over the edge of the lake of sea water which had slowly formed about his feet. He knew very well what Felznick meant when he said "assignment." Johnny wouldn't see New York for months. He'd be shot from spot news to spot news, always on the go, worn out. . . .

"Got a swim out of it anyway," he muttered to himself, climbing into the small studio car.

Chapter Two

JUPITER banged into Mars and eighty police sirens shrieked down the Milky Way, while Johnny embattled Neptune, warding off the wicked trident with the Empire State Building. And all the while, the captain of the SS *Birmingham Alabama* was suspended in mid air, banging Johnny on the head with a bung starter and weeping softly, "I told you so. I told you so."

"Oh, my head," groaned Johnny, swimming up through murky depths to arrive at last in the bedroom of his Long Island apartment, mutually shared with Irish.

A patch of chill on his brow startled him and his lids sprung up to behold, not Neptune, but Irish sadly messing with an ice bag.

"How's that?" said Irish.

"Heaven," whispered Johnny, closing his eyes again.

"What happened to you? Where'd you go? How come you went on a bender? You never did that all this year. Was everything all right? You come in with the help of a cop and a taxi driver, crying, 'All is lost! All is lost!' I paid the bill. It was thirty-nine dollars and twenty-one cents. What'd you lose?"

"Please," begged Johnny, pulling the sheet up over his face.

"Where'd you go?" persisted Irish. "How come all is lost?"

"Will you go away?" said Johnny.

Irish went away, but he came back—bringing a tumbler made up of tomato juice and red pepper and Worcestershire sauce. There was a determined gleam on Irish's small face. In a moment, before Johnny knew what had happened, Irish had thrown the contents down his throat. Johnny yelled. He opened and shut his mouth like a dying fish. And then, seeing that no flames were shooting out of his throat and that he had not exploded, he sank back into the pillow.

"Now what's lost?" said the merciless Irish. "What'd you do?"

Johnny gazed hopelessly upon his helper. He felt too weak to throw a pillow at him and shut him up. With a weary sigh, Johnny said, "We're in the soup." He thought about it for a while, gradually remembering just why they were in the soup, and then he added, "No pictures. They'd all been soaked in sea water when the passengers took to the drink. That's it. There wasn't one good film in that batch, and you . . . let's see . . . you didn't get a shot of the ship from the air."

"Gosh," said Irish in mortified recollection. "Gosh, I forgot. I . . . I was so scared you'd drown, I didn't think about that hand camera."

"You'll never make a cameraman," said Johnny sadly, overlooking the fact that Irish had been one for years. "You gotta think about pictures, nothin' but pictures and only pictures and . . ." he subsided. Finally he turned over with a curse. "To hell with pictures, to hell with everything. I make one bull in seven years and I get it hot and heavy. I'm going to quit. That's what I'll do, I'll quit. It's a lousy life. Two hundred and fifty a week—for what? For tryin' to get yourself

killed. Two hundred and fifty a week to take pictures! To hell
with the pictures. I never want to *see* another picture as long
as I live! You hear that, Irish? I never want to turn another
crank! I'll buy a chicken ranch, that's what I'll do. I'll buy a
chicken ranch and do like that salesman said. Two chickens
will get you a million three hundred thousand in two years.
That's the life. No more of this hell and glory. No more of this
gettin' up in the middle of the night rushing off to trouble.
Trouble! That's what it is! News is trouble, and nothin' but
trouble. I'm through. I quit. I'm sick of trouble. . . . Gimme
that phone!"

Irish, with grimly compressed mouth, gave him the phone.
It was a direct wire and he snarled, "Gimme Felznick . . . That's
what I said. Gimme Felznick and tell'm this is Johnny Brice."
With a ferocious scowl, he eyed Irish. "I'll tell him what he
can do with his job. Two hundred and fifty a week for tryin' to
kill yourself. I'll—" His gaze lighted upon a basket of flowers
on the bureau behind Irish. "Where'd those come from?"

"Dunno," said Irish. "Here's the card."

Johnny looked at it. His brows contracted and he paled.
"Read that!"

Irish read, "To Johnny with all my love in appreciation of
giving me such a lovely scoop; Bert Goddard. PS Don't forget
you borrowed a hundred off me last night. Love and kisses."

Irish was about to swear, but he heard Johnny at the phone.

"Yes, Mr. Felznick . . . No, Mr. Felznick. Where? Idaho?
But my gosh, Mr. Felznick, how . . . But I . . . Yes, Mr.
Felznick." He hung up, and dared Irish to say anything. "Get
something packed."

"Where we goin'?" said Irish.

"Idaho. Ninety-thousand-acre forest fire, three towns cut off from the blaze. . . . I knew it. I knew it. He's picked the farthest place he could find, that's what he's done, the old—" And then he saw the flowers. "Love and kisses! Wait'll I meet that guy Goddard! Just wait. G'wan! What the hell are you standing there for? Get something packed."

Irish looked embarrassed and backed away from the door he had started through.

Johnny started to speak luridly, but stopped, startled to behold a lovely young lady in his silk dressing gown. She came almost timidly to the threshold of the room.

"What—?" began Johnny. And then, "Oh, so it's you again, is it? Why don't you go home?"

Unable to thoroughly appreciate that she was getting the brunt of the rage felt against Goddard and Felznick, she backed up at the snarl in his voice. She wasn't at all sure of herself or her welcomeness, and her eyes grew suspiciously bright.

"I . . . I haven't any place to go. I can't go any place! They'd get me. Don't send me away. Please, Mr. Brice, don't throw me out. I'll be awful good. I'll keep your place clean and cook your meals. I'll be careful and not get in your way. And I won't eat much, honest I won't."

Johnny realized that he had been very rough and that he was making himself look like a brute. And so he got rougher, because it made him mad. "I don't care what you do, but get out of my sight. You . . . you damned Jonah! That's what you are, a Jonah! I pick you up and make the first bull I've made in seven years. And now what? And now I've got to go to Idaho and mebbe get burned up in somebody's lousy forest fire. I never had any bad luck until you came along." Again he realized that he was taking out his utter wretchedness upon her, that he was using her for an alibi for his own short-sightedness in not examining those films. And because it made him hate himself, he roared all the louder. "Beat it, and let me die in peace!"

Irish squirmed. "He's upset, that's all. Maybe we better go." And, so saying, he pushed her out of the door.

Johnny glumly swung out of bed and stumbled to his shower. The cold water hit him like bullets and he gloried in the pain of it. But, while he rubbed himself down, he gradually smoothed out his temper and dwindled down to muttering only an occasional, "Idaho!"

He ate the breakfast Irish had had sent up from the restaurant below, stabbing at his fruit as though it was Felznick. "Publicity hound," he growled. "Idaho!"

He drained his coffee cup, and when he set it back he noticed with detached interest that there was a note under the saucer. He pulled it out and read it.

> Warning. If you don't get rid of that dame and stop hiding her, you'll be pushing up daisies.

He blinked at it and read it through again, to make sure he wasn't seeing things. He turned it over, pondering upon the identity of the sender.

Irish brought him to himself. The pint-size was standing in the door with a grip in his hand.

"Look at this," said Johnny.

Irish looked at it with knitted brows. "Who do you suppose sent this? Who'd be after that girl, huh? Maybe we better ditch her."

"What?" said Johnny, getting ugly again. "You make me sick. What kind of a guy are you, anyhow? Somebody threatens you, so you get scared of your shadow. Haven't you any guts? Somebody wants to knock off that girl. Huh, I'd like to meet 'em."

Irish scratched his head in wonderment. "You couldn't be figured out by Einstein," he decided. "One minute you tell her to get out, and then as soon as she gets like dynamite, you want her to stick around. Contrary?!"

"Shut up," said Johnny.

The girl was in the door again and Johnny looked at her, frowning. "You ever been to Idaho?"

"Why . . . no."

"You're goin'," said Johnny. "Got any clothes?"

"No."

"Irish, go buy her some clothes. . . . No, wait. That'll never do. Look, somebody might see you buying them. This place might be watched."

"Watched?" said the girl.

Johnny got up and handed her the note. She gave a start and her eyes grew very round. She swallowed convulsively. A moment later she had composed herself.

"You're Irish's size," said Johnny. "And your hair is short enough to put under a helmet. Irish, go get her some of your clothes."

"You mean you'll take me to Idaho?" she said, with relief.

"Who's after you, and what's this all about?" demanded Irish.

"I . . . no, I can't tell you. But you've got to be careful. They . . . they would do anything."

"What the hell are you bullyin' her for?" Johnny demanded of Irish. "Go get her some clothes, and stop runnin' off at the mouth." He took up the phone and got the airport wire.

"Run out the cabin job, Steve. We're headed for Idaho."

Chapter Three

ROARING westward, Johnny Brice had ample time both to look at and wonder about this strange girl who had so suddenly become a part of his existence. When they stopped at Chicago, she was under great tension, eyes constantly roving the field and striving to appear unconcerned at the same time. That she labored under a heavy nerve strain was very apparent when they took off once more and she sank back into her seat, exhausted.

After that Johnny watched her intently from his seat across the cabin, letting Irish do most of the flying on the excuse that he, Johnny, was going to attempt some night shots of the vast forest fire which stretched along half a mountain range and imperiled—so the radio said—some five thousand lives if the wind changed. But that would all take care of itself in due time, and it would be soon enough for him to start worrying about saving their necks and getting the pictures at the same time.

He watched the girl, pretending to sleep, so that she would not again mask her real self. He was taken, now that he studied her, with the delicacy of her features and the smallness of her hands. Her honey-gold hair was delightfully real—and Johnny knew henna when he saw it and appreciated not seeing it. In turn, oblivious of his regard, she watched the country unroll below them, small ripples of pleasure going through her at the variety of colors of the checkerboard earth, of the dollhouse towns, always with their guardian church spires; it was apparently all new to her. She watched their shadow striving mightily to keep up with them, hastily leaping hedges and ditches, highways and hills. Still believing herself unobserved, she pulled the table around on its hinged brackets and took up the pencil there, writing slowly on a scratch pad, pausing now and then to look at the faraway earth, pencil poised against her lips and then writing again. It went on for some time, and finally Johnny's curiosity got the better of him. He stood up quietly, but an air bump made him clutch his chair. She caught the motion and, in a flurry of embarrassment, wadded the paper into a ball.

"Let's see it," said Johnny.

She shook her head, tightening the wad. He reached out his hand, but before he had reached her, she had already lowered the window an inch and the white ball fled back and away.

"What were you writing?" said Johnny.

"Nothing."

"You might at least confide in me. I have some rights."

"It wasn't anything," she said, cheeks turning a deeper hue.

"It must have been," said Johnny.

"It . . . it was some poetry," she faltered.

He looked her askance and sat down, changing his attention to the Black Hills which slowly rose out of the horizon ahead. She pushed her hands down into the pockets of Irish's flying jacket and studied Johnny.

"You don't believe me," she decided at last. "Maybe you thought I was framing a message or something. But, honest, it was poetry. This is the first time I have ever flown over the United States."

"Why don't you give me a break?" said Johnny. "I'm on your side."

"You weren't this morning," she reminded him.

"Aw, can't a guy blow off the steam of a hangover if he wants? And besides, it was funny that I'd pick you up and have my first bad luck in the movie business all at one and the same time. Give me a break. What's your name and who's after you, and why? I got influence, sometimes."

"You . . . you couldn't ever help me out of this . . . but then, I've said too much already."

"Is it some smuggling outfit?"

"No."

"Maybe it's espionage."

"N-No."

"Maybe it's the police."

She didn't answer, and he showed immediate interest. "Are the cops after you?"

"There's no use trying to find out. It would be worth your life to know."

"I've got some rights," persisted Johnny, with a slow smile. "After all, when you pick up a ship at sea, you got rights. And I picked you out of the drink. Salvage, that's what. I've got salvage rights on you. And you won't even tell me your name."

"Don't make me tell," she pleaded. "It . . . it would be the end of you."

Johnny considered her calmly. "Something on the order of Medusa, eh?"

She was startled.

"Oh, cameramen can read, too," smiled Johnny.

"I may be a Medusa, but perhaps you aren't Perseus."

"I don't want your head," said Johnny, "and I doubt that you'd turn me to stone. I only want to know what's in it."

"Does the right of salvage include that, too?"

"It does," said Johnny, "but definitely."

"Then, someday, if I live, perhaps I'll tell you." And that was all she would say.

Chapter Four

A GAINST the evening sky they could see the rosy glow of flame and before they had traveled much further, even at this height the smoke began to sting their eyes. And then, as they climbed, the whole earth below, it seemed, was one vast blanket of flame. To the north, like lightning, the crown fire was running. To the south the dead earth smoldered.

The girl stared down, appalled, feeling small and weak before this panorama of seared mountains. The drone of their engine seemed small and when the heat currents began to buffet their wings, knocking them about the sky, her heart stood in her throat, lest they be thrown down to cook in this hell. It was hot enough at three thousand feet.

Steadily Irish flew onward.

"How's the gas?" said Johnny.

"Enough for a half-hour," said Irish.

Johnny looked down. "There's plenty of this. Think you can find a town and field in all this smoke?"

"Maybe, if it doesn't get much darker."

"Locate the field, if you can, but give me a break. I'm going to turn a crank on this."

She watched him coolly set up and check the load of a DeVry. Irish was going up higher so they could get a better shot. She began to be nervous about the gas, about the possibility of finding a place to land in that angry expanse which stretched illimitably below their frail wings. The bumps lessened as they went higher.

"Might not have another chance," said Johnny practically. "Might rain or something, and spoil the news." He was turning his crank, eye fixed to a sight, tripod hugged against him to keep off some of the engine vibration. "Boy, this is a shot. Wish it was color. See those blue flames? That red sky . . . ? Boy!" His enthusiasm increased as he cranked. "Higher, Irish!" His eyes gleamed as he looked around for angles which would show the most flame. "Boy, we're lucky. They might have put this out."

Five thousand people and a hundred thousand timbered acres, she thought to herself.

"Wouldn't it make some picture if we could get one of those towns burning?" said Irish.

"None of them are," said the girl.

"But they might," said Johnny hopefully.

"But where would we land?"

"We'll worry about that when we get some of these pictures. Take her down, Irish. Got to get that crown fire. Might see some of the fighters from the air. Got two of them that were trapped, once," he told the girl. "But no such luck this time."

She shuddered, clutching the sides of her chair as they dived sickeningly down at the geysering flame below.

Johnny lined up the crown fire as it sped from treetop to treetop, one giant, terrifying path as far as they could see to the west.

"Got it?" cried Irish.

"Got it. Locate the town!"

Irish pulled back on the stick and they shot upward, out of choking smoke. But they did not go far. With a jarring cough, the engine missed a beat. And then it repeated in a swift succession of volleying backfires which sent a plume of red-blue flame out of their exhaust stack under the wing.

Irish put the nose down. The engine stopped entirely and all the sound there was came from below. It was a roar like surf, and the girl knew, with terror clutching at her heart, that that sound was the crown fire racing above the forest.

"Ahead or behind?" said Irish.

"Ahead. Find a brook. Find anything." Johnny's hands were swiftly taking the load out of his camera, rolling it up and wrapping it up. He seemed to have no attention for anything else.

"There's an open space!" yelled Irish. "Belt yourself down. This is going to be rough!"

"Throw your belt across you," ordered Johnny, sinking into a chair and buckling his own.

She found that her hands were frozen. Somehow she managed to fasten the clasp. It was too loose for her and she glanced at Johnny. He was still wrapping up the film, using his own coat.

"Might get singed," said Johnny, tapping the drum in his hand.

She had barely heard him when they struck. She didn't know what happened. She lost a few seconds out of her life and knew nothing about them except that they had gone. She was sitting in her chair, but her weight was all against her side. In the angry red light which permeated the forest, she could see the trees, all horizontal about her. Hands grabbed her and jerked her out of the ship.

"Where's a creek?" yelled Johnny.

"I saw something shiny over to the left!" yelped Irish.

She could hear a snarling, angry sound to the south and knew that it was the crown fire. Her legs failed her and Johnny scooped her up, running and stumbling through the grass, guided by Irish's white jumper.

Deer, with death in their eyes, bounded through the clearing, failing to notice either humans or a terrified cougar that sped in their midst. Small animals, badgers, squirrels, chipmunks and a lumbering bear fled blindly from the greatest devourer of all—FIRE.

Johnny half-slipped, half-leaped down a clay bank. A beaver dam had crossed this creek in former years but, though its builders were dead, water still remained there, several feet deep. Into it plunged Irish, up to his waist, and then she saw that he gripped the big moving-picture camera in his arms. The whole world had slowed down for her. Animals in a steady stream cleared this creek and raced out of sight into the darkness beyond. A wise chipmunk plunged in. Against the scarlet sky she could see legions of birds striving to outstrip the smoke. There was something grandly beautiful in this drama of death and only the shock of the water broke her momentarily detached state.

Johnny had thrown her down. "Swim up under one of those mounds!" he cried. "There's air in them. Gimme that camera, Irish."

Into it plunged Irish, up to his waist, and then she saw that he gripped the big moving-picture camera in his arms.

"Gee whiz, this ought to wow 'em!" cried Irish, ducking into the pool.

"Lay 'em in the aisles!" cried Johnny, opening wide his lens. For a moment he was conscious of the smallness of his voice against that crackling roar which sped upon them and then he was again all business, wading into the pool until the water was up to his neck, holding the camera at face level. The tripod helped buoy it up. He reached over and snatched the helmet from the girl's head, putting it on and drawing the goggles down.

They heard the plane catch fire. A moment later it exploded and then, after that, all the sky was alight. The crown fire, traveling with a plane's speed, whooshed over them. But as an undertone, the girl could hear the steady whir of the camera, focused now upon the trapped animals, now up the scourged trees. Burning brands rained upon them, hissing as they struck the pool, setting fire to the brush on the banks. Johnny swore abruptly, but the whirring camera sound went on.

She was conscious that she held the film he had taken from the plane and knew she had been holding it up carefully for minutes. It surprised and pleased her to find that she had been calm all that time, despite the heat which penetrated the beaver mound.

Suddenly she heard Irish scream, "LOOK OUT!"

There came a long, groaning sigh, a swish of branches and then a numbing crash which sent the water over the mound in a great wave. Something struck the girl's head and she fought to keep up above the surface but, gradually, she sank down.

She had no consciousness of being moved, but when she

again opened her eyes, it was to behold Johnny's blackened face. He had two white rings around his eyes where the goggles had been, and a long wet streak of red which worked slowly down his cheek. It was scorching hot and the world glowed redly, flickering from small flames which still licked the trunks of the dead forest giants. The pool was a dirty mess of floating charcoal and dead, small animals. A powdery ash was snowing around them, gently and quietly, throwing everything out of proportion for her.

"She's alive!" said the singed Irish.

"Yeah," said Johnny, hiding his own relief. It seemed funny to her that he should want to smoke with all this eddying about him, but he was lighting a cigarette. He sat down in the shallow water over the dam, remorsefully puffing as he stared at the devastation. She lifted herself up a little and saw that a great tree divided the pond. Others had fallen up stream and down, their roots already unstable in the soft earth and needing only the furious blast of the crown fire to knock them over. It had been this, then, which had struck her.

"Did you get the pictures?" she said, sitting up.

"The air shots are down there some place," said Johnny, jerking the cigarette to indicate the bottom of the pool. "You dropped them when you went out. The camera is likewise in the drink, the whole top knocked out of it."

"The tree didn't hit you?"

"Missed me—a whole foot," said Johnny.

"They're all gone," wept Irish, unashamed. "They're all gone. And they was such swell pictures. Animals and the crown fire, and everything."

"Can't you salvage them?"

Johnny didn't even bother to answer.

"But maybe just plain water—"

Irish moaned, "Please."

Johnny touched his cheek and looked at his bloody fingers in some surprise, deciding he had better wash his face. He knelt down, dabbling in the water.

"It's going to be a hot walk," he said, "and maybe a damned long one."

Irish recovered himself. He took out a pocket knife and approached a dead deer sprawled on the bank. The girl looked away, already too conscious of the smell of singed hair and burnt meat which hung over the world about them. However, a little later, when Irish finished roasting the steaks on a stump, she took her portion.

Johnny was looking at her critically as he ate.

"What's the matter?" she said, acutely aware of her smudged face, torn clothes and wet hair.

"Lady," he said slowly, "I hereby christen you 'Jinx'."

Jinx

Chapter Five

TWENTY tragic hours later, the scorched, ragged, blackened, wretched, hungry, weary, dispirited, footsore and homeless trio trudged into Coeur d'Alene's best hotel, cast off by a Forest Service truck. For a long, long time it had been raining and the soot had clung to them, a black scum overlaid by gumbo.

The clerk was startled and then dismayed at the pools of black paint which were tracked across the floor—and though he was not at all haughty about costume, he considered this a shade too much for two men and a boy to so scandalously appear in his hotel. He drew himself up behind his desk. "I am very sorry but we have—"

"Skip it," snarled Johnny, flashing a wallet with his World News card before the fellow's face. "You're giving us three connecting, your very best. Where's your telephone?"

The clerk amended his first lack of hospitality. He called, "Front!" and a bellhop came forward, with misgivings about any tip. "Mr. Brice of World News," said the clerk, "will occupy the governor's suite. Here is the key. Will you go right up, sir? I could have some food sent to you in your room. You can use the phone there, and we have some haberdashers in Coeur d'Alene who are up to the minute. Were you filming the fire? Was it as bad as they say?"

"Send up the menu, three portions of everything," said Johnny.

They got into the elevator and were taken to the top floor. The boy was oblivious of their footprints on the carpets. His eyes were roundly fixed on Johnny, and he fell all over the rooms as he opened windows and made a pretense of checking the towels.

Johnny said, "Tell them to put a dollar on the bill. And get me some Scotch."

"Oh, no, sir. I mean that's all right about the dollar. I always wanted to be a cameraman. Do you suppose—"

"I said a bottle of Scotch," said Johnny.

The boy, still goggle-eyed, retreated.

The girl sank spiritlessly into a chair, pulling off the helmet. Her hair had been protected and the bright honey-gold of it was in startling contrast to her black face.

Irish walked straight into one of the bathrooms and stepped under the shower without bothering to take off his clothes. A muddy Mississippi ran down the drain and his small bright face began to show through its camouflage.

Johnny threw his stained self down on the silken bedspread and wrapped his fingers around the phone. "Gimme New York, Bryant 9-3300. I'll hold on." He sat there listlessly, hearing the round whir of sound which shot his call through to Chicago, then to New York. He heard the buzz of the ringing at the office. "Felznick. This is Brice." He got Felznick. "This is Johnny. I'm in Coeur d'Alene."

"You got the pictures?" said Felznick eagerly. "One of them towns almost burned! Did you get it?"

"Sure I got it. I got everything. I got aerial shots at dusk, and then the engine choked, when the smoke got too much for the carburetor, and we smeared in right ahead of the crown fire."

"You get the crash?" said Felznick eagerly.

"Sure. And then I got the animals heading out from the blaze, and then, with water up to my neck, I got the crown fire leaping over this creek we stumbled into."

"Johnny, you are a genius! A genius! You can come back to New York. I raise your pay! I always said there never was such a cameraman . . ."

"Wait," said Johnny. "A big tree, afire, fell down right across the pool and smashed the DeVry to smithereens and knocked out the . . . knocked the other can into the drink. I haven't got a single shot, not even the remains of the burn."

There was silence at the other end of the phone. And then there was a long, heartfelt sigh.

"I did my damndest," said Johnny. "That was all I could do."

"Brice," said Felznick. "Brice, I am being calm. I am being very cool, Brice. I am not going to say more than this. . . ."

"I quit!" said Johnny.

"The hell you do!" screamed Felznick. "You're fired! A twelve-thousand-dollar plane, and you lose your pictures! You're fired. I never want to hear of you, see you, speak to you! Never! I won't pay your bills! You can sue for your pay and to hell with you! Don't ever come close to me again! Never!" There was a bang as he slammed the phone on the hook.

Johnny hung up slowly, looking at the girl. "How do you feel?"

She gave him a game grin. "Okay. A little hungry."

"Eat hearty," said Johnny. "This may be our last meal, and we may have to wash dishes for that."

"You mean—"

"I'm fired. Irish is fired. We're in the soup, Jinx." He got up and walked into Irish's bathroom, stepping over the edge of the tub and joining Irish under the shower. The lampblack fell from him in inky waterfalls. Irish sat on the edge of the tub, wringing the water out of his coveralls.

"We're fired," said Johnny.

Irish gave a start as though he'd been shot. His mouth hung open and he stared straight ahead. "Fired?"

"And no pay," said Johnny.

"What'll we do to pay our hotel bill?" gulped Irish.

"You figure it out."

There came a knock on the door and the girl hastily put on her helmet and answered it. Three waiters began to move five tables, all snow-white-napkined and groaning with food, into the room. The bellhop had a stack of boxes in his arms.

"The haberdashers sent these up with their compliments," said the bellhop. "Some silk bathrobes and stuff. Gee, I bet it was awful hot up at that fire."

She didn't dare speak and betray her woman's voice and so she only smiled and happened to glance down. The bill was protruding from under a plate and the figure on it was so heavy it showed through the back. Thirty-nine dollars.

A waiter gravely took the slip and handed it to Johnny under the shower. Johnny signed it and the man withdrew.

"You got any money, Irish?" said Johnny.

"I got five bucks."

"I got three," said Johnny.

"You got the company check book."

"Think I'm a crook?" said Johnny.

"Sometimes I ain't so sure," said Irish.

Johnny saw the girl in the doorway. She was holding out two silk robes and slippers and pajamas.

"They're free—in hope of future trade," she said.

"Huh," said Johnny. "Put them on the chair and close the door."

"I'm going to my room and bathe," she said, hesitating. And then, "Johnny... do you think, maybe... that I'm really a jinx?"

"Well?"

"It wouldn't be the first time," she said, sadly closing the door.

A moment later there came another knock and Johnny stepped out of the tub to string a river across the main room. Two young men in snap-brim hats and unpressed clothes were there.

"Mr. Brice?" said one.

"Right," said Johnny.

"I'm from Associated Syndicate and this is my pal Tom ... I mean this is Mr. Thorpe, of United Service. We're holding down the local desks. We got the idea we might fill our wires with you. They're through talking about the fire since this morning, and now we've got to keep up the human interest. You know how it is."

"Sure," said Johnny. "Come in."

They seated themselves on the sofa and Johnny stood in

the room, shedding blood from the wound on his head and sooty water from his torn and charred coveralls. He knew what kind of picture he made, and he didn't even offer to go clean himself up before he talked.

"I hate to talk about it," said Johnny. "In all my career, I have never been so close to death. Can't you boys excuse me and—" he got out the bottle the boy had brought and filled two glasses half full of Scotch, presenting them, "and just say a cameraman crashed a couple minutes ahead of the crown fire and was lucky enough to get out alive, even though he risked his neck to get the greatest pictures ever filmed and they were spoiled by a falling, flaming tree which struck directly across the camera? Haven't any wish for publicity, gentlemen. After all, we're in the same racket. News is trouble and that's all there is to it, and if us newshawks lose our lives trying to serve the headlines hot, then World News, United Service or Associated Syndicate still goes on, regardless."

They drank. Simpson, of Associated, sat very still. His face was working oddly. "Pretty damn heroic, ain't it, Thorpe?"

"Oh, nothing like that," said Johnny. "I was just doing my duty and I failed to get the pictures, that's all. It doesn't matter how I failed. I did fail. And, boys, I don't really want to talk about the way the plane exploded—"

"I hate to insist," said Thorpe, restraining his eagerness, "but couldn't you do a fellow newsman a favor? Just the rough details. We'll fill them in. After all, we've got a wire to fill. Human interest following this great fire, the worst in history. You know. And you saw it right in front of you."

"But—" protested Johnny, dripping sooty water.

"Just as a personal favor," said Thorpe.

Johnny took a slow drink and gave them another half tumbler full apiece. "Welllll, if you put it that way, all right. We were flying just over the crown fire, well knowing our engine might quit. It was all part of getting the pictures for World News. And so there we were, singed by the raging heat below, not knowing if we would ever get away alive when the engine quit! A chill raced up my spine as I realized the horror . . ."

They sat enraptured, recalling themselves to their pencils only with great difficulty, and the longer Johnny talked the louder the flames roared until the words "World News" and "duty" began to ring synonymous in the minds of the two reporters.

At last the bottle of Scotch was empty and so was Johnny. Mopping the sweat of creation from his brow, he said, "And that's how it was. Now if you'll pardon me—"

"Gee, I got to get this on the wire!" they both said in unison. They hardly stopped long enough to pump his hand and then they were gone.

Johnny went back to his bath and found that Irish was all decked out in a yellow silk robe five sizes too big for him. "Gosh," said Irish, "ain't I beautiful?"

"All you need is some cheap perfume," said Johnny. "I fixed it, for the minute. That yarn will break in the local rags as well as on the wire, and then maybe they'll stretch the credit."

He bathed, and when he girded himself in his red bathrobe and stalked forth, he found that Irish and the girl had already laid waste to two tables. He wrapped his hands around a whole chicken and began to gnaw. "You guys make me sick," he said around white meat. "You eat like a couple animals."

There came another knock on the door and Irish bobbed up to answer. It was the manager, with the clerk hovering worriedly behind him.

The manager adjusted his glasses. "Mr. Brice—"

"That's him," said Irish.

"Mr. Brice," said the manager, "it pains me to inform you that we are in receipt of a wire from your New York office stating that your World News checks are not to be honored. You . . . have, I . . . er . . . ah . . . infer . . . lost your position."

"That's right," said Johnny. "Paramount upped a pay figure higher than World, and so I changed over. My Paramount checks won't be here for a couple days, but meantime, I've got plenty of money. I'm surprised that you would be worried about such a trivial thing. Here, I'll get my wallet if you don't believe me. I—"

"Oh, no, no," said the manager, hastily. "I didn't understand. . . ."

"Quite all right," said Johnny.

The manager bowed out, and Johnny took another chunk off the roast chicken. He looked fixedly at the girl and she avoided his eyes.

"Have some more chicken or arsenic or something, Jinx," said Johnny. "Irish and me have got eight bucks between us and you're going to be put on a bus as far as that will take you."

She wept a little but very quietly and then went off to her room.

"You're a brute!" said Irish.

"And she's a jinx!" snarled Johnny.

"She likes you. She told me so."

"To hell with what she likes!" snapped Johnny, attacking a steak. But a moment later, "What did she say?"

"She said she thought you weren't near as tough as you acted. She said . . . "

"Shut up," said Johnny. "She goes, and that's the end of it!"

Chapter Six

IT was very early morning—a time of day abhorrent to newsreel cameramen. Johnny awoke and did not know why except that he had a feeling that he had somehow done wrong. He fished aimlessly around the dressing table beside his bed, almost dislodging the phone. That near-accident served to bring him more clearly to himself and he propped himself on one elbow while he found his pack and lighted a cigarette. He was used to waking up in strange quarters and so his surroundings told him nothing. He yawned and massaged his curly brown hair. He looked over at Irish, who slept in the other twin bed, completely lost in a tangle of covers and grinning idiotically in his sleep. Johnny wondered if he had had a row with Irish, and then decided against it. No, something else was bothering him. Yes, he had been fired, but that didn't seem . . .

The Jinx, that was it. He'd told her to get out, come morning, and now morning was here. That was it; and he lay back, puffing ferociously at his cigarette. He was in his rights to make her beat it. Hadn't had a bit of luck since she had happened into his life. He was glad he'd see her no more.

And then a small voice within told him, "You can't trace a single bit of your bad luck to that girl, and you know it.

It was your own damn fault that you bought water-soaked film on that ship. It was your own orders which made Irish go down too close to that crown fire; you might have known that your engine would quit, in all that smoke."

"Yeah," muttered Johnny, "but just the same, I never had hard luck before."

"That's why," said the small voice, "you had so much good luck you thought you were perfect, and so you stopped taking precautions about things. You were the best flying cameraman in the business and you always got the pictures. World News couldn't get along without you. Yahhhh!" jeered the voice. "See how easy you were fired? You didn't amount to so much. Guys like you grow on every bus."

"Aw, lay off," growled Johnny to himself. "That doesn't prove anything. I was going good until the Jinx came along, and just as soon as she leaves, things will be going good again. Wait and see."

"Yahhhh!" said the small voice. "You're nutty. Things won't go good until you settle down to your job again. You were flying too high, that's all. You just don't like the girl."

"I do," said Johnny. "That's the hell of it."

"I suppose you can find girls as pretty as her anyplace."

"I wish that was true."

"I thought you said she was bringing all your bad luck and there you are trying to fall in love with her."

"Who, me?" snapped Johnny.

"But that's all right. You won't be worried about her long. Probably somebody will read that newspaper story and know

54

just where she is and as soon as you turn her loose, they'll be picking her up in an alley with a bullet in her back. But that's all right, she's a jinx! Yahhh!"

Johnny sat upright in bed. "I don't believe it!"

"That story will get all over the shop. Whoever is after her will be able to trace you and then get her."

"That's her hard luck!" snapped Johnny to reinforce his flagging courage.

"Whatcha talkin' about?" complained Irish.

"G'wan back to sleep," said Johnny.

Irish looked at the clock and then gave Johnny an accusing stare, afterwards wrapping the blankets around his head and burrowing down for another snooze.

Johnny sat holding his knees and puffing on his cigarette. A knock, very light, sounded upon his door, and he growled, "Come in."

She entered cautiously and he saw with some wonder that she had washed out the white flying suit and helmet and had dried them with some magic or other. Further, she had transformed her appearance with methods beyond Johnny's ken. She didn't look like a boy, despite those overalls. For the first time since that morning she had suffered the impact of his hangover he saw her without disguise. The helmet dangled from her hand and her honey-gold hair poured down over her shoulders like beaten metal. Her lips were full and red and sensitive and her eyes were soft and blue. She stood just inside, as though afraid he would throw something at her.

"Well?" said Johnny, trying to keep up his resolve.

"I came to tell you that I was going."

"Goodbye," said Johnny.

His tone hurt her, but she made no sign. "Is that all?"

"What more do you expect . . . Jinx?"

"Johnny . . ." She paused.

"Well?"

"Johnny, why do you act so tough? You aren't that kind of a guy. You just put it on to keep people from seeing that you aren't. You don't have to do that, Johnny. Gosh, I never knew anybody that had the personality you've got—if you'd only use it."

"Look," said Johnny, hit harder than he dared show. "It is too early for a lecture out of Lord Chesterfield. You said goodbye."

"Not yet," said the Jinx. She reached into the pocket of her overalls and pulled out a small wad of bills.

"What's that?" snarled Johnny.

"I had this in a money belt and I don't need it—not now. There's two hundred dollars here—"

"I don't want your money," said Johnny, working very hard now to appear as ungracious as possible, lest he break down. "Buy a ticket for Europe or Chile or some place."

"I've saved enough for a ticket and some clothes."

Johnny's voice was a threatening monotone. "If you don't put that money back in your pocket I'll break your neck."

"But . . . but I lost you your job, Johnny. I brought you bad luck. . . ."

"Nuts," said Johnny. "Take your dough and get out of here, before I lose my temper."

She hesitated and then, afraid of his scowl, she put the money back. She edged out of the door. "Goodbye, Johnny. I hope . . . maybe you'll have some good luck now."

She was gone and he sat staring at the door and feeling terrible. Why did he have to act that way to her? Wasn't he human? Was his soul turning into a mass of celluloid? He got up and threw his cigarette out of the window.

"Well!" She was gone and he ought to feel relieved. She was dynamite—and she was a jinx.

But no matter how many times he repeated it, he could not make it quite ring true and could not keep himself from wanting to call her back and apologize.

The ringing phone saved him. He picked it up and barked, "Hello! Johnny Brice speaking."

The smooth, purr on the other end alarmed him. As soon as the operator had said, "Here is your party, sir," Felznick said, "Oh, hello, Johnny."

Johnny was upset. Felznick calling this time of day—and then he recollected that it was noon in New York. "Hello," he said cautiously.

"How are you this morning?" said Felznick. "Rested up, I hope."

"Yeah," said Johnny.

"And how is Irish? Fully recovered, I trust?"

"Look," said Johnny with great patience. "Either you're crazy or I am. The last time I talked to you, I was fired."

"Oh, that!" said Felznick, with careless dismissal. "I was upset about my wife. You know, they found Louise in Paris. She didn't sail."

"Who is it?" hissed Irish. "Paramount?"

"Shut up. . . . No, not you, Mr. Felznick. Glad to hear your wife is safe."

"Yes, yes, a great relief, Johnny, especially since I got no publicity out of it. And, by the way," he added, falsely casual, "that was good going on your crash story. Made page one in all the New York sheets. Had the angle, you know. Give your all for pictures and then lose them. Good stuff, Johnny. They had you slated as dead yesterday, after you failed to turn up for thirty hours."

"I see," said Johnny.

"Now if you're all rested up," said Felznick, "you might run down to Frisco and catch the China Clipper. You've just about got time—"

"Wait a minute," said Johnny. "Maybe I want to stay fired."

"Has Paramount been after you?" said Felznick, severely. "Haven't you any loyalty? Is this the thanks I get for teaching you all you know about the business? Now I'll—"

"But—" began Johnny, out of honesty.

"I don't care about any buts. I'll up your pay. How much did they offer?"

"They—"

"All right, I'll make it three hundred a week, but not one cent more, and up Irish to two-fifty with a recording rating. But not one penny more!"

"All right," said Johnny.

"Now, follow me closely. Harrington was wounded yesterday in the fighting up on the Amur, which means I'll have to replace him. You're furthest west, and the only one close enough to the Clipper to catch it in time. And you got another break. The Chinese ambassador-at-large, Mr. Sen Shu Wu, will be aboard that plane. The Japanese would give anything to get his treaty papers and you might witness some sabotage or an attempted murder or maybe even a murder. Think of that, Johnny! You stay right beside Mr. Sen Shu Wu, and if anything happens to him, put it in the can! I'm depending on you, Johnny."

"Look," said Johnny, "is this an assignment, or a scheme to get us bumped off?"

"Hah hah!" laughed Felznick. "Always the wit, eh, Johnny? Now pick up some cameras in San Francisco, and don't fail to connect with that Clipper. Everybody gets bad breaks sometimes, and you've had yours. Now we can count on you, I know. Good luck, Johnny."

Johnny hung up and Irish looked searchingly into his face. "Did we get it?" said Irish.

"Pay raise," said Johnny. "You two-fifty, me three hundred. Boy, what an assignment this is!" He sighed deeply and then, shaking off all extraneous thoughts was immediately business itself. "Roll out! We got to get some clothes. If we're going to make that Clipper, we'll have to step on it!"

"Gee," said Irish. "China! I wonder if those Japanese left anything at Mum's. 'Member that big tall Russky? Maybe she's still there, Johnny. Think so? Gosh, I been prayin' we'd get a crack at that fighting. Bet we can get some swell shots. Maybe get some air-raid stuff, up close. Maybe, huh, Johnny?"

Johnny walked toward the bathroom. He stumbled and grabbed his foot, swearing. When he looked down he saw that a rock was the offender, and he almost kicked it again before he remembered that he was in his bare feet.

"Wonder where that came from," said Irish.

"Somebody must have thrown it in from the fire escape," said Johnny, picking it up. "Look, there's a note on it."

Irish read it aloud, from under Johnny's arm. "'Brice; Take a friendly tip. You're monkeying with dynamite. If you don't believe it, tip off the cops—any cops—that you're harboring Jacquelin Stuart, and let them take her off your hands and collect the reward besides. Your own office could tell you about her if you'd only call. Stop being a damned fool and turn her in. If you don't, I'll have to take other measures, not so pleasant. A Friend.'"

Johnny crumpled the note angrily.

"Gee!" said Irish. "The cops! Say, Johnny, what you know about that? She's wanted. Maybe for forgery or counterfeiting or smuggling or something. Huh? What do you think, Johnny?"

"Shut up."

"But look, Johnny. It's plain as day. This gang wants her, see? She double-crossed them and they tipped off the police that she was guilty, and now they're scared to contact the cops again. And if they bump her off, she bein' a criminal, nobody will ask too many questions. Look, if we don't turn her over to the cops, they'll try to kill her!"

"She's a jinx," Johnny was saying bitterly. "She leaves and my luck changes. She's a jinx and I'm through—"

"You mean she's gone?" gaped Irish.

"Yes, she's gone!" yelled Johnny wrathfully. "Don't stand there gawping at me! Do something! The kid's in trouble. You want to let the cops get her, huh? You want her to swing for something she maybe didn't do? Get hold of her! Try the airport and the bus station! Don't stand there like a fool! Get going!"

"But I only got this yellow bathrobe . . ." wailed Irish.

Johnny booted him through the door.

Chapter Seven

MR. SEN SHU WU had the kind of a smile that is painted on dolls—with the exception that nothing could ever remove it, not even breakage. He answered all questions with the very best of polite language, bowed in payment for every attention and generally gave the impression that he had but one mission in life—to utterly efface himself. At this time in particular he was anxious to be as unnoticed as possible and, when he thought no one was looking, his small brown eyes would try to reach around corners as though expecting, from moment to moment, the arrival of at least a tiger.

Johnny, after seven years of photographing mankind in action, was not likely to miss any such signs, and before they had shoved off from San Francisco, he had already remarked to Irish in private, "I hope you can swim."

"Huh?" Irish had said.

"Yeah, swim. But what I'm worrying about is not whether we'll be lost along the wayside, as that's pretty well established, but whether Mr. Sen Shu Wu will have company on the highway back to his ancestors."

"Gee, y'think there'll be trouble?"

When the big Clipper wallowed down the bay to swoosh into the sky and head westward, the Jinx asked the same question. "What's the matter with our friend, Johnny? He looks like he expected the sky to fall in. Is there going to be trouble?"

Johnny looked at her grimly and she knew what he meant.

"I suppose there will be," she decided, with a sigh. "But you don't really think I'm a jinx, do you?"

Johnny leaned back on his head, dragging on a cigarette and scanning the vanishing coastline below.

"You don't, do you, Johnny?" she persisted. "Honest, things just happen, that's all. You . . . you'd have turned me over to the police if you really thought I was."

"I don't know why I didn't," said Johnny. "Why don't you come clean with a guy? What did you do?"

She was instantly frightened, glancing around to see if any of the other passengers had overheard.

"All right," said Johnny. "Keep it to yourself." He looked at her speculatively, still asking himself over and over just why he considered it his bounden duty to play escort to her. She was lovely—especially so in those gracefully tailored whites she had mysteriously produced in San Francisco—and there was something . . . No! He was too damned tough to get caught falling in love with any girl. He'd been too far and seen too many. And besides, wasn't she a jinx?

Mr. Sen Shu Wu, across from Johnny, smiled faintly and looked a little green. He was getting airsick, despite the calmness of the day, but he didn't allow himself to be discomposed. "Nice sea, isn't it, Mr. Brice?"

"Yeah," said Johnny, "there's lots of it."

"Very strange, seeing the coast depart behind us. Makes

one feel oddly without purpose, sailing off into the horizon. It is so very far to my country."

"It's plenty far to swim," said Johnny.

Mr. Sen Shu Wu's eyes flickered over Johnny's camera which, at Johnny's request, had been left in the cabin. He said nothing, but he knew very well that this newsreel man was not there by accident. Beneath his own feet was a small briefcase—but size had nothing to do with importance, as treaties take but small space, and a fifty-million-dollar bill of exchange can be wadded into a vest pocket. The enemy would do anything to get Mr. Sen Shu Wu personally, let alone to stop those treaties and that bill.

Mr. Wu and Johnny smiled at each other, understanding with mutual respect.

"News consists mainly of disaster," commented Mr. Sen Shu Wu.

"News is trouble," said Johnny. "And quantity makes quality."

"I hope, for your sake," said the Oriental politely, "that you are not disappointed. As for me . . ."

Johnny saw the doom in his eyes and tried to cheer him up. "Never mind. I've got a bad-luck charm here that makes it completely impossible for me to get any good news shots. You're as safe as if you were home in bed."

"That might not be so safe," smiled Mr. Sen Shu Wu. "Are you referring to your charming companion?"

"Twenty-one-carat jinx," said Johnny. "This trip will be as uneventful as taking the Albany night boat."

Mr. Sen Shu Wu's smile was a trifle uncertain for a moment.

"You newsreel men astound me, Mr. Brice. Have you no regard for your own safety? An attack upon me would inevitably place you in extreme danger."

"He eats it," said the Jinx, "with or without cream. His idea of heaven would be the assassination of the president with siege guns during a five-alarm fire in an earthquake. Newsreel men have cameras for hearts, Mr. Wu."

"Aw, they do not," stated Irish, turning around. "I saw Johnny drop his camera in a flood once to pull three kids out of the drink, and he damn near drowned doing it, too."

"He probably already had his pictures," said the Jinx.

"Sure," said Johnny, before he thought.

They laughed at him, and the big Clipper bore upward into the smoother air and the Pacific stretched limitlessly below. Hawaii was far ahead, and beyond that . . .

Chapter Eight

B UT nothing happened in Hawaii and the endless blue leagues of the Pacific fled by below, flanked by the strange, castellated clouds of the tropics, which flamed each night before the sea vanished below and flamed each dawn before the sea could again be seen. Always the clouds, never overhead, rarely below, always on the horizon. Forever the sea, that seven million square miles of the Pacific, a wide, variegated world of its own, too great and lordly to notice the bright wings of the airliner.

And then Manila, a week out of San Francisco, a week in the company of men one would never see again, but who had become friends just the same. The Jinx, moving in a world she had never before seen, riding the crest of great events, had seen deeper into Johnny than he knew.

In the sticky-hot Customs, she clung close to Irish and Johnny, recoiling at the sight of the armed, brown police, anxious to be free once more of these patrolled towns. Even more than the officers, she was interested in the changing crowd, especially when it contained well-dressed people.

And then they were aloft again, heading for China. But it was no longer a Clipper, but a small, eight-passenger cabin plane of the Chinese National Airways.

It was now that Mr. Wu's calm began to break. Any sudden remark would make him start violently, and forever his eyes patrolled the skies ahead and above. Out from under them rolled the South China Sea and, finally with morning, China spread before them. Their destination was Chau-chow on the Han River, a prudent choice of Mr. Wu, who hoped against hope that the—

Japanese battle planes glittered briefly as they wheeled in the sky. The pilot, a young American, gave a startled glance into the cabin and then peered upward again. Mr. Wu, face pressed against the window, shivered like a deer which has heard hounds. There were eight of those planes, vicious and stubby and efficient. They were here with a job to do, and with Oriental calm they set about it, getting neatly into a stair-step formation out of which they would start their dives. A sharp, brief barking sound was in the air—those pilots were warming up their machine guns for the coldblooded kill.

The Jinx's face was pale, eyes fixed in fascination upon the death which waited in the sky. It seemed impossible that such cool deliberation could forerun what it would. The pilot of the passenger plane was diving, engines wide open. Below was the Han River, its bulk broadening, as they neared it, into a coffee-colored sheet. Suddenly the Jinx was aware of Johnny's activities. With steady hands he was checking the load of his camera. Irish was reading a light meter and counting it off. Johnny lifted the camera to the heavens and the small whir of it was audible, even above the scream of the transport's engines and the growing yowl above.

A rattling, snapping sound burst about them. A great hole

appeared in the back of the Chinese secretary's neck. He quietly folded up on the back of Mr. Wu's seat. Daylight could be seen in the top of the cabin; small holes were there, like stars. The rattling sound came again. But the Jinx heard Johnny's camera whirring once more. He was shooting the river as it swept up to them.

Past the windows flashed, in rapid order, four of the Japanese planes, wheeling below to zoom once more into the sky while the remaining ships came down.

The transport's engine clanked and was still, and the dismal howl of wind past struts and through bullet-holed wings was suddenly more than the Jinx's ears could stand. The drumming engines of the battle planes seemed far off and unreal.

The transport leveled out for a crash landing in the water. The camera's whir stopped for a moment, while Johnny buckled his belt. And then he pointed the nose of his camera up once more and caught three warplanes streaking down, one after the other, emptying their drums and flashing by. Swiftly he turned his lens on the water which, in the next instant, shot over them in a great, translucent sheet. The transport bobbed up, plowing ahead. All about them the water was lined with rows of small geysers. Machine-gun bullets. The *cha-cha-cha-cha* of the guns was louder now. The transport was slowing down. With a start, the Jinx saw the black bulk of a man-o'-war looming just ahead.

The pilot leaped up. "Swim for it!" he shouted, as he slammed open his door. He was gone. Mr. Wu struggled up, death stamped like a white mask on his face. He went through the port into the water below.

69

The transport leveled out for a crash landing in the water.

"Beat it!" ordered Johnny. "Grab her, Irish."

Irish grabbed her and thrust her out, breaking her instinctive hold on the plane. The water was cold as she fought through its depths, and then Irish had her again. They swam swiftly away from the ship.

Suddenly she knew Johnny wasn't with them. The water was boiling around the plane as bullets hailed out of the sky. In a sick surge of terror she screamed, "Johnny's back there!"

Irish turned in the river and stared at the transport. And then they saw Johnny. He had just finished his last shot of the man-o'-war and was turning his camera on the struggling Mr. Wu, now far out from the ship.

"Johnny!" she cried.

In the din of guns her voice was lost. In an agony of suspense, she watched him coolly take out the drum and wrap it in a rubber sheet, thrusting it into a container. But even then he did not jump. With the plane rocked by striking lead, Johnny was calmly loading his camera again. Finally he focused it on the man-o'-war, the sky, and then the water, and then he dropped it and, in a long dive, hit the water.

The pilot had vanished. Mr. Wu was struggling feebly and then she knew that Johnny wasn't coming to them, he was heading for Mr. Wu. With unceremonious hand he gripped the ambassador's collar and towed him toward the shore.

The shelling had stopped, and the resulting quiet was hard on the eardrums. The shore seemed a thousand miles away, and she began to despair of their ever reaching it.

Suddenly, directly in front of them, a ship's boat loomed.

Brown hands fastened themselves upon the swimmers and lifted them into the boat.

The Jinx pushed her hair from her eyes and looked around at the Japanese sailors on the thwarts. Johnny, she saw with a start, was empty-handed. No, Irish did not have the drum. With her spirits sinking even lower, she felt the conviction that she was again the cause of lost film.

Mr. Wu was nodding politely to a Japanese officer, who bowed politely in return, and then the gig swerved into a long turn and sped back to the man-o'-war.

They clambered up the black side, trailing water on the white-scoured ladder, and arrived in a group of polite officers on the deck. The captain, seeing them, turned and made a sign with his hand to the gig, which curved outward again and swept down upon the wrecked but floating transport. She saw the officer retrieve Johnny's camera from it, while others tossed luggage into the gig and then the boat came back.

"I am very sorry," said the bedraggled Mr. Wu to the Jinx, "to be the cause of unpleasantness to you."

She didn't think he meant more than the transport crash itself, until she heard Johnny talking to the captain.

"Ah, yes," said the captain to Johnny. "I am very sorry. I realize how serious it is. But, believe me, we made a most regrettable mistake, thinking you were a Chinese bombing plane sent to destroy this warship. Very regrettable, very sorry."

"A common mistake, Captain," said Johnny, tight-jawed, but not to be outdone in politeness. "If you would be so kind as to set us ashore—"

"The country," said the captain, "is very wild. I would fear for your safety. May I invite you to be my guests?" He was eyeing the camera, which was being brought aboard. "We will store this for you—if you do not mind?"

"Oh, not at all," said Johnny, grimly.

"You will be taken to your cabins," smiled the captain.

Escorted by a young officer, Mr. Wu went slowly down a hatch and out of sight. Another officer signed that the Americans were to follow him. Johnny took Irish and the Jinx, each one by the arm, and tagged the officer.

"The dirty rats," said Irish. "That pilot didn't have a chance. He's dead on the bottom."

A thudding explosion shook the river behind them and the Jinx glanced back to see that the remains of the transport were pattering the breadth of the river.

"If we get out of this," said Johnny, "we'll be lucky. Keep your chin up."

"You mean . . . they won't set us ashore?" said the Jinx.

"Us?" said Irish scornfully. "Newsmen? Ready to blast that story across the world? What do you think would happen to Japanese prestige if it got noised around that they attacked an American plane, killed the pilot, took Mr. Wu a prisoner and executed him?"

She looked at Johnny.

"Sure, his goose is cooked. They'll ease his body over the side as soon as they get to sea."

"But they can't hold us forever!" she protested.

"No?" said Johnny. "That's like the jailbird saying they can't jail him—but there he is. Keep your chin up. I hope you'll like Japan."

"When I think of those pictures," mourned Irish, "I wanta cry. The biggest scoop of the war this year—on the river bottom." And he glanced at the girl and she saw in his face that he was beginning to believe things about her too.

As they entered the large cabin suite they heard the anchor engines grinding, and through the port they saw the river bank begin to slide away. For a moment the Jinx was a little dizzy.

"Is . . . is this business always like this?" she said.

"Like what?" said Johnny innocently.

"One minute in the Atlantic, the next in the mountains and . . . I can't believe it . . . here we are in China, and heading for Japan and all in less than two weeks."

"Yeah," said Johnny, disinterestedly lighting a cigarette, graciously offered by the ship.

She had just started toward her cabin when the door burst open and two marines stepped aside to let the stick-bristled captain enter, followed by a lieutenant.

"We are very sorry," said the captain, politely. He made a sign and the lieutenant approached Johnny, who at first drew back and then submitted to the inevitable. The lieutenant made a quick search and, from under Johnny's belt, where it had lain flat against his stomach, drew out the film container. They then searched Irish without result.

"Thank you very much," said the captain. "We have that film left in your camera and now this. My field glasses are very fine, very powerful. Thank you very much." Bowing courteously, he withdrew.

Johnny's lean face was strained. He looked fixedly at the girl.

She winced and quickly closed her door, but not soon enough to block off his "Jinx!"

Chapter Nine

THE ship plowed through the soft dark of the Eastern Sea, phosphorus curling in straight lines away from the bow, a small slice of a moon paving the water with silver squares. Within four or five hours, and still before dawn, they would dock at the Japanese port.

The Jinx rested against the rail, looking down at the sea, her thoughts a turmoil of misery but, for all that, looking very lovely in the softness of the night. She became aware of Johnny standing beside her and she made an effort to rally. "It's lovely, isn't it? If . . . if only I knew what was going to happen, I might be able to enjoy it more. I've never been in the Orient until now."

Johnny dragged thoughtfully on his cigarette. "Well, if that's all it will take to make you happy, I can tell you all about it. We're going to be held incommunicado until hell freezes over. We know too much about Japanese methods in general and the sinking of an American-owned transport in particular. They know what the US press would say about the murder of a pilot and Mr. Wu."

"You mean Mr. Wu—"

"Sure. He's been dead for more than a day. He tried to escape, they said." He tossed his cigarette into the water. It glowed in a bright arc on the way down and then, suddenly, was extinguished and gone.

"But they can't do that to us," she protested.

"No, they may not kill us, but they'll imprison us—which, as far as I am concerned, is just as bad."

"But our ambassador—"

"Will never know a thing about it," said Johnny.

"But they can't do it!"

"In almost every country of the world," said Johnny, "there must be imprisoned at least one foreigner, long ago given up for dead, held merely because he knows too much. Russia, France, England—"

"And the United States?"

"Who knows?" said Johnny.

"Then maybe we'll be held for years and years! Oh, Johnny—"

"Keep your chin up!" he said, almost savagely.

She wavered, tried and then succeeded. "I'm sorry, Johnny."

They stood in silence for some time and then heard footsteps approaching. It was the captain, smiling, hissing and bowing.

"Good evening. We come to Nagasaki very soon now. I regret that I shall be forced to deliver you over to other agencies. Is there anything which I can do?"

"You've done quite enough," smiled Johnny. "We appreciate your kindly hospitality. But there is one favor I might ask."

"Yes?"

"You might," snapped Johnny, "give me those pictures back and let me go free. You'll never succeed in covering this up. How do you know that pilot didn't get away? Must you add crime to crime, and hold neutrals prisoners? What if the world hears about that?"

"The pilot," said the captain, sadly, "was mistaken by our airmen for Mr. Wu and was sent, I trust, to his fellow birdmen in heaven. I saw him sink. It is to be regretted. Military expediency, Mr. Brice, is a God difficult to serve. There is one thing I can do."

"What's that?"

"Naturally you are interested in your pictures. They are very excellent. We have, of course, complete facilities aboard, and we took the liberty to finish them. It has become customary for us to record our activities, and perhaps foreign works and vessels, wherever possible, and we are indebted to you for your aerial views of our diving battle planes. We can learn much from them. The technique of our pilots was most ragged and, with the aid of your pictures, may be pointed out. Perhaps, if you would like to see them—"

"It's the sadist in him," growled Johnny. "All right, I'll look at them."

"It is I who offer the favor," quietly reminded the captain.

He led the way down into the officers' salon where, copying the fashion of the United States Navy, motion pictures took up part of the burden of morale. After the evening show, the projector was still in place and the captain rang for the operator. With some pride he indicated the projector.

"It is much different from the day of the samurai, eh, Mr. Brice? Japan has come far. Our Navy is every bit as modern as your own and, who knows, may some day be as large."

The operator came and went away again to bring back

Johnny's film. There was no positive print, only the negative, and though black and white were reversed, making the diving planes like weird ghost ships against a black sky, the excellence of the photography was apparent even to the Jinx.

Johnny sat very still. He watched the planes coming down, watched the water coming up, saw his shot of Mr. Wu's secretary getting hit, witnessed the testimony of his own news sense in every foot of that film. It was all there, the man-o'-war, the ship's gig, the rising sun insignia on the warplane wings. It was, he knew, the action shot of the year, done in brilliantly clear photography. As the film whirred out, he felt a little sick at his loss, realizing that, in his pride, he had forgotten it for a moment. He heard the operators clattering the reel into its flat can and then gathering up all his equipment.

"Lovely, eh?" said the captain.

The Jinx stifled a sob. She knew what Johnny was thinking and feeling. She got up and started toward the hatchway at the rear of the salon, dabbing at her eyes with the handkerchief. The operator failed to see her, and his arms were so loaded that he failed to realize his course. He bumped her and the cans clattered in every direction. The ship was rolling so that many went far, and the sailor, with one tortured eye on the captain, hastened to pick them up. The Jinx was quick to help him, stacking the cans into his arms. The operator glanced at that most precious of the containers—Johnny's—to make sure it was still there. Then he stumbled out into the passageway and was gone.

Johnny went up on deck, following her. They stood at the rail once more.

"If I'd had a chance like that!" snapped Johnny. "You dope! Why didn't you try to grab that can?"

"He checked it. It wasn't any use. You saw him look at it. Besides . . . I felt so bad . . . I didn't even think—"

"Bah!" snarled Johnny. He was aware of Irish standing morosely in the dimness. "You know what happened? She had her hands on our film and didn't even make an effort to steal it!"

Irish looked sadly at the Jinx. "There's one thing you've got to learn in this business," he said. "If we was all honest, how do you think we'd ever get any pictures?"

"I'm sorry," wept the Jinx.

"We couldn't have gotten away with it anyhow," said Johnny, feeling guilty for taking out his rage on her. "He looked at the container to make sure. Oh, well," he sighed, "it's been a long time since I saw Nagasaki."

Chapter Ten

THE Jinx awoke in frozen terror, well knowing that somebody was in her room. She would have screamed if a hard hand had not bruised her lips.

"Shut up!" whispered Johnny. "We're in Nagasaki. The anchor just went down and we're waiting for dawn to dock."

She saw that it was still dark.

"Get dressed, and make it snappy," said Johnny.

She heard him close the door and knew he was waiting on the other side. She slid out and got into her clothes without turning on a light. She was both frightened and hopeful by his manner.

A moment later she stepped into his room. Irish leaped up off a bunk, his dark eyes blazing with excitement. Johnny doused the light and cautiously opened the door into the passageway, while Irish took the Jinx by the arm and steered her after him. Only small blue globes were burning in the tunnel of steel. No one was in sight. Johnny cautioned them to silence and crept onward.

They had reached the door that led to the deck when Johnny stiffened and, sweeping back his arm, slammed his companions against the steel and held them there. A Japanese marine, betrayed by his white bands, was standing just beyond.

Johnny's hands slid slowly outward. The sentry moved

and Johnny jerked back. Once more he advanced, and then grabbed for the man's arms and mouth. The marine dropped his rifle, but Irish caught it before it could clatter to the deck.

The darkness of the floor gave forth struggling sounds and the Jinx supposed that Johnny was having a difficult time subduing the sentry. It seemed to take much longer than it should have, and she began to breathe swiftly as she momentarily expected them to be uncovered by another guard. No marine had been far from them so far on the trip, and now they were in port, it was certain that they would be put in less easily escaped confinement, if found wandering at this hour.

She almost cried out when she saw the Japanese marine stand up in silhouette against the lights of the shore, which could be seen through the open door. But it wasn't the marine.

Irish stepped out to the deck, glancing all around. He walked confidently across the planks to the rail and paused there, casually examining the lights ashore and the water below. He moved along, pausing now and then while Johnny and the Jinx held their breath. An officer came down a ladder and passed Irish, who recalled himself in time to refrain from saluting. The officer disappeared into a companionway and then Irish beckoned stridently to Johnny and the Jinx.

Silently they rushed to the rail and saw a bumboat below. It had a lantern burning, but the boatman was asleep atop his wares, waiting until the crew and dawn found him.

Johnny went down the side, gripping the painter. When he stepped on the foredeck of the bumboat, the movement startled the Japanese awake. Johnny dived across the cargo and the clean crack of his blow came faintly to the deck. He put on the straw hat and coolie coat, to make his silhouette better, and then lifted up his arms to receive the Jinx.

The rope slipped in her fingers and burned them. But, uncomplaining, she came down to the deck of the bumboat. Irish was instantly beside her, slashing the painter with the purloined bayonet of the sentry.

Footsteps were sounding on the deck and Johnny batted out the bumboat lantern. The footsteps ceased, while the bumboat drifted with the current down the side of the warship. It bumped into others, similarly tied, whose occupants muttered irritably, half asleep, while Irish shoved away from them.

Suddenly from the deck there came a ringing shout. Johnny seized the sculling oar and the water boiled around the blade. The bumboat shot out away from the man-o'-war and lunged toward the bright lights of the docks far away.

They had no idea exactly what was happening. They heard commands being fired and, once, a wail of pain, which indicated the sentry's chagrin. But they had not found out yet that the prisoners were not still aboard the ship.

"You're too soft," whispered Irish, working another oar. "You shoulda dumped him into the boat with us."

They were no longer steering toward the docks. The Jinx saw a cluster of colored lights on the starboard and guessed that would be their destination.

Minutes passed with painful slowness, and the warship's outlining lights grew farther from them. Abruptly long blades of light reached into the heavens and stabbed down to sweep the water.

"Pull!" pleaded Johnny.

"I've worn out both arms already," grunted Irish.

The lights came nearer and nearer, and then Johnny whispered, "Get down, both of you!"

They ducked, feeling the bumboat turn in a swirl of foam. Johnny took more time with his stroking on the sculling oar. He was drifting back toward the warship now and, by putting no strength into his work, still kept it far away. The searchlights caught the boat and held it. Johnny put up an arm to keep the light out of his eyes and eased up on his work. The lights went away and then, as though to catch any trick, again focused on the bumboat. But Johnny placidly approached the warship. The searchlights went elsewhere, not concerned with one of many such craft, doubtless on its way out to sell fruit to the sailors.

A swift heave on the oar almost tipped over the boat and Johnny snapped, "Let's go!" He turned, and they again darted toward the colored lights.

After minutes, each one hours long, they neared their goal. The Jinx could see the shape of a cross outlined in lights on the ground, but it was not until they grounded on the concrete of a ramp, and square buildings loomed above them, that she understood that this was a seaplane base.

Johnny sloshed into the water and then he and Irish lifted out the girl. Johnny pushed a bill into the boatman's hand who stared stupidly at what was, to him, great riches. Johnny made a motion with his fist and pointed out toward the warship again and the boatman jumped willingly to his sculling oar and made off.

They went on cautious tiptoe up the ramp toward the hangars. Lights were shining within and the sound of wrenches and hammers came to them above the mutter of voices. The silhouette of a great plane stood against these lights. It was a bomber, destined for service on the Chinese front and being put in readiness for a dawn takeoff.

The Jinx was afraid that Johnny might attempt to attack these mechanics. There were too many of them. They swarmed over the wings, trailing long gas hoses, checking equipment, testing struts and engines.

The trio pressed into the shadows of oil drums and crept closer into the hangar. Once they had to cross an open space and the Jinx was certain that they would be seen, in the light now as they were. But with the blinding small bulbs in their hands, the mechanics saw nothing.

In a moment Johnny was under one of the great wings, pressed against the cart which carried the hull of the seaplane down to the ramp.

They lay there, hearing men walk over their heads, and waited for something to happen. Shortly, it did. The warship, convinced at last that the quarry had flown, turned on siren and whistle full blast to call all signalmen in the harbor to their posts. Launches were darted away from her hull and the whoop-whoop-whoooooop of the insane siren seemed to drive them away.

"They'll comb this town!" whispered Irish.

Johnny signaled for silence, though nothing could have been heard in the bedlam of that black harbor. The mechanics, curious as to the disturbance, leaped down off the wings and ran out on the ramp to stare at the cruiser, now dimly seen in dawn.

"Quick!" said Johnny, squirming out from against the truck and leaping to the cabin door. He boosted the Jinx inside and almost threw Irish after her.

"You can't take off!" said Irish. "They'd have fighters in the air! These engines—"

"Grab that wheel!" snapped Johnny, throwing his palms down on the starters and throttles.

There was no time for Irish to change his mind. The engines ground stridently and then caught with a roaring blast which shivered the hangar. Staring over Johnny's shoulder through the front ports and down at the ramp, the Jinx was amazed to see that the mechanics only glanced back, and then looked forward once more. They were too intent on the ship's siren and the flashing messages to read anything but an early arrival of the plane's crew into the sound. Johnny nursed the throttles. Irish wanted to shout with glee at the stupidity of the crews.

But they were not allowed more than two or three minutes of grace. A petty officer, suddenly realizing that all was not well, trotted up the ramp toward the ship, frowning concernedly up at the turrets.

"Now!" cried Johnny, slamming all guns ahead.

Four engines, too cold to be even, crashed out, their crescendo swelling up, up, up, until the truck began to move down the rails which led into the sea.

The crews turned, staring at the moving monster, unable to believe that it was really moving, despite the testimony of their eyes. And then they leaped to the right and left off the tracks, and threw themselves flat to escape the wings.

Down the track the plane sped to hit the water in a sheet of spray, engines still full on and warming with each passing second. The flying boat wallowed as it plowed through the small waves, gradually rising up higher and higher in the water, until it reached its step. They were skimming across the harbor through dim, gray light, and both Johnny and Irish whipped the controls right and left to avoid bobbing bumboats. Their speed made all the harbor blur, and then they were no longer crashing in the waves, but flying smoothly over the warship they had so lately quitted—the officers of which had no way of knowing that here went their quarry.

Johnny yelled, "What's happening at the seaplane base?"

The Jinx fumbled down the bomb racks until she came to a cross-barred turret, which startled her by swinging with its guns. She looked back at the beach to see a searchlight popping off and on, as its shutter blinked out a strident message.

"They're signaling!" she cried.

Johnny hauled back on the stick. "Stall or no stall, baby, you've got to grab yourself some air."

"She's only making a hundred and eighty, full gun!" cried Irish.

"What do you want for a nickel?" shouted Johnny.

Belatedly the warship had the message. Two of its sister cruisers, already awakened by the siren's din, also had the message. An antiaircraft gun far behind them slapped a ball of fire into the air. Others crashed immediately after it.

Johnny left the controls to Irish and struggled back beside the Jinx, to stare through the turret slits at the harbor, so swiftly falling away from them.

"There they go!" he cried, and the Jinx followed his finger to see the two plane catapults on their warship's deck belch white smoke as they were fired. For an instant their planes were going too fast to be visible, and then they bobbed down toward the water and, with engines roaring, began to streak upward.

"On cold engines," said Johnny. "Those guys have got guts!"

The two Navy planes were fighting for altitude and, for the moment, were left far behind. Johnny's seaplane bomber roared mightily as it curved upward, taking a course eastward.

"Get forward," ordered Johnny, taking the machine gun in his hands. Clumsily he fumbled for the loading handle and then pulled it. A moment later the gun stuttered and the belt began to churn through the breach. It was a .50 caliber Matsubi.

The Jinx, deafened by the roar, went back to Irish. He gave her a grin, and she saw with a shock that he was truly delighted to be in the middle of such a scrape.

Johnny's gun kept rattling. Overhead an engine screamed and another series of barks was in the air. Johnny bellowed directions to Irish and the big ship heeled over for a moment. The Matsubi fixed itself upon the nose of the diving Nakajima and let go. The tracer laced a spider web around the Japanese pilot's head and he pulled up, startled to find opposition.

The other ship dived and Johnny gave it its medicine. No one knew better than Johnny that he could not hit the sea below, much less a moving plane, but these pilots had great respect for a Matsubi. They had fired the .50 caliber slugs themselves. They drew off from the flying fortress, having no way of knowing how well manned it was, and not half as anxious to greet their ancestors as the government would have other governments believe. The flying fortress itself was impregnable to a pursuit plane. They were sure of that. They had been told it often enough.

Johnny watched them hang on some thousands of yards astern. The bomber was going into the rising sun, which came swimming out of the mountains ahead and in a few minutes would be shining for them out on the Pacific. Pursuit planes were not likely to love the idea of going straight on out to sea.

Johnny relaxed as he saw the Pacific reaching endlessly ahead. Yes, the pursuit planes were turning back to Nagasaki.

What a shock the Army boys would get up in Alaska when a Japanese bomber came roaring into their choicest Aleutian harbor. What a shock!

And then Johnny's smile sobered as he thought of what his own reception would be. There wouldn't be anything for it this time—he was through.

Chapter Eleven

THE Army boys were embarrassed, if privately amused, and were suspiciously eager to get Johnny Brice and party out of the Aleutians as swiftly as possible, so that the bomber could be quietly restored to Japan and no questions asked. Accordingly, an Army bomber sped southeastward, via Anchorage, to Seattle where, at Boeing Field, a very discouraged Johnny alighted, his face falling after he had thanked the officer pilot and the need for forced spirits was done.

"Aw," said Irish, as they rode in a taxi into urban Seattle, "the worst he can do is fire us."

"Yeah," said Johnny. "But news gets around. Three times is a charm, Irish, and just between you and me, the movie industry, when it hears about it, won't be having much to do with Brice and Company."

They got out, from force of habit, before the largest hostelry, the Olympic Hotel, and Johnny dug up change for the cabbie. The Jinx began to be uneasy, scanning the crowds restlessly, and very anxious to be out of public view. She had a premonition that something was going to happen, and when they entered the lobby and a bluff, derby-hatted individual stopped and gaped at her, she straightened up like a soldier about to face the firing squad.

"Hey!" said the thick-faced one. "Hey, you!" And he charged toward her.

Johnny was instantly aware that nemesis had overtaken the Jinx and while he might take refuge in superstition, there was something in him which sprang up now with a maul fist and knocked the big guy kicking.

"Help!" bawled the detective, struggling up. He surged in toward Johnny again and once more the fist connected. *"POLICE!"* screamed the detective, once more bouncing to his feet. Johnny set himself for a finishing blow and, suddenly, felt his arms seized from the rear. A patrolman had him, the house detective had Irish and the copper had the Jinx.

"Come on, you," said the copper, dragging the girl away.

"Jinx!" wailed Johnny. "Wait a minute!"

"Goodbye, Johnny," she wept. "Goodbye, Irish."

Johnny lowered his head to struggle and then, finding the patrolman's grip too sure, looked up again. But she was out of sight. Bleakly he stared at Irish and, feeling no fight, the patrolman let him go.

"Y'gonna be good?" said the patrolman, "or do I run you in? Grady gimme the sign to let you go, but I ain't so sure."

Johnny straightened up his bedraggled coat and, with Irish, walked back to the street, escorted by the house detective. The two stood there for a long time, and Johnny finally walked to a drugstore and called the local precinct. Yes, Grady had reported in. No, no information. No, the girl was leaving immediately for the East under escort. Yes, no, couldn't give out any information. State Department business, maybe.

Johnny looked at Irish. "Maybe she wasn't a jinx, Irish. Maybe I'm just a sorehead."

"Whatcha gonna do?" said Irish.

"We're taking the next plane for New York. We got a scoop for the papers on that China thing anyway. Maybe we can argue Felznick into taking us back. . . . Naw, no chance. But let's go, anyhow. She'll need us."

Two days later, Johnny and Irish, still looking like something out of a grab bag, walked hopelessly into Felznick's office. He wasn't at his desk and so they sat down, waiting, Johnny so distrait he almost forgot himself far enough to start to light a smoke, violating the one necessity of a newsreel office, where celluloid begs for a spark. He recollected himself just as Felznick entered.

"Hello, boys," said Felznick.

"He don't know," thought Johnny. "Chief, we got into a little trouble. It wasn't exactly our fault, but we couldn't fight the whole Japanese Navy—"

"With nothing to fight with," supplemented Irish.

"—and what's done is done. We got a news scoop for the papers—" he cleared his throat nervously, "but the film—"

"Oh, that!" said Felznick, surprisingly. "Jack, come in here!"

Irish and Johnny, wondering who Jack might be, looked at the doorway. A moment later there appeared a person who scintillated, a person one hardly ever found off Park Avenue, the finished product of all beauticians and the best dressmakers. In silk and fur and lovely leather, smiling upon them, stood the Jinx.

Johnny gaped. He leaped to his feet. "Hey! Am I crazy or—?"

Felznick looked startled and then grinned. "Maybe you haven't been introduced properly. Brice, this is Jacquelin Stuart, otherwise Jack, my much-abused stepdaughter. I admit I have been wrong about her. She has always maintained that she could learn this business if she had a chance and I've always said it was no place for a girl. And when I told her last month that she was crazy, she took advantage of those reserved cabins on the *Kalolo* to come back and protest by getting a job with some other outfit. She wouldn't let me know. Now, is what she says straight? Is she savvy enough to learn the business?"

"Good gosh," gaped Johnny. "But I thought the cops—"

"Since she ran away," said Felznick, "and especially during the past ten days, I've been bombarding the country with her picture. Her mother was wild, thinking she was dead or something. How about her ability?"

"Why . . . gosh . . ."

Jack's eyes pleaded with him. Jack's eyes told him that she had braved the waves of the Atlantic, fire, bullets and jail to see what it was all about.

"Sure," said Johnny.

"Gosh, yes," said Irish, echoing Johnny's choice.

"Johnny," whispered the Jinx to herself, as though she had voiced a prayer of thankfulness.

"Now that's fine," said Felznick. "I never thought she had the guts. Maybe it's because I didn't like her old man. But she'll get the outfit anyway, so I might as well act like I feel—pretty happy that she proved her point. By the way, boys, do you want to see your pictures? They're being fixed for today's release, rush stuff—special billing and all that."

"Pictures?" gaped Johnny and Irish as one.

"Sure!" said the Jinx, to cover up their surprise. "Sure they want to see their art. What a silly question!"

Johnny dazedly stumbled into the projection room and the Jinx almost had to hold him up. "How in the name—?" said Johnny.

"I changed those containers, dummy," whispered JackJinx. "I slammed our reel in place of one of theirs and theirs in place of ours, so the box he'd marked would be heavy. I stuck it in my jacket front and later lashed it around my waist. Surprised?"

"You bet," sighed Johnny as he sank into a chair. "You saved my neck."

"And you saved mine."

"But those threatening notes!" he whispered, puzzled.

The Jinx leaned very close, her cheek against Johnny's.

"I wrote 'em," she whispered back. "To make you think—"

The lights went out and the reel flickered to the screen. It ran through its entire length, and then Felznick, forgetting Johnny had taken them, crowed, "How's that for a scoop! There's drama, there, boy! Drama! That's news, the kind of service we always deliver. World News is always first. We crash it before the papers. A real scoop! It's got everything. . . ." By that time the lights popped on and Johnny suddenly found his collar too tight.

"You weren't listening!" said Felznick.

"Oh, yes, he was!" grinned Irish. But he didn't add to what.

Story Preview

NOW that you've just ventured through one of the captivating tales in the Stories from the Golden Age collection by L. Ron Hubbard, turn the page and enjoy a preview of *The Battling Pilot*. Join pilot Peter England, whose humdrum airplane routine is unexpectedly disrupted when his company reassigns him to transport some special passengers. But when his aircraft gets attacked by a mysterious fighter plane, Peter realizes he's transporting dangerous cargo—a princess seeking to turn the tide of a war!

The Battling Pilot

PETER ENGLAND sat brooding over four throttles and a wheel. His eyes went restlessly from left to right and right to left, taking in a couple square yards of meter-studded panel, watching oil temperature on Engine Three, revs on Engine One.

A thin little fellow slid quietly into the copilot seat beside him. England glanced in that direction with some annoyance. "Huh. You're Tom Duffy. What—"

"On deck, Captain. I've been promoted to Number Ten," said Duffy, trying hard to hide his elation.

"Where's Nelson?"

"Sick list."

"You ever fly a kite?"

Duffy blinked. "Why, I've been copilot here for three years, Mister England."

"No time to break in punks. I've been on here for sixteen."

Duffy looked sideways with some misgiving. Pete England was top pilot on the line, a long, hard-jawed devil, moody as Atlantic weather.

"You bet," said Duffy. "Some day I hope to be tops."

"Don't," said England bitterly. "Nothing in it but grief."

"Grief? Why . . . I thought it was fun, scooting from New York—"

"New York to Washington," said England. "Washington to New York. New York to Washington. Washington to New York. Lots of fun. You must be in a spin."

"Oh, no," said Duffy, his round face glowing. "I think it's swell. Keeping up the tradition—"

"Tradition," snorted England.

"Sure, tradition. You're the idol of—"

"Of what?" snapped England. "The passengers? Hell, you'll be telling me this job is romantic in a minute. La-de-da. You're a punk."

Duffy blinked and squirmed in the bucket seat.

"You're dumb," added England, as an afterthought. "A guy would have to be dumb to like this."

"B-But you're tops!"

"You've got to get on top to look back, don't you? Fun! What kind of fun is what I'd like to know. New York to Washington. Washington to New York. Flying a kite. Lugging sixteen passengers north for a lunch date, sixteen passengers south for a session with Congress. What kind of fun is that? I know every silo from here to New York. I know every spot on every cow. I can take a bearing on the number of milk cans sitting outside a gate. What's the fun about that?"

"B-But gee!" said Duffy. "You don't seem to realize what an honor it is—"

"To what? Cart sixteen passengers around, and half of them airsick? 'Mister Pilot, please don't hit the bumps so hard.' Damn the passengers. Maybe ten years ago this was romantic. But that was ten years ago. There was some element of danger then. Not now. This is as common as pushing a locomotive from Podunk to Punkin Center. If it wasn't for the pay, I'd have quit long ago. Say, what in hell is keeping those damned passengers?"

Duffy looked down the tunnel made by the awning and saw a group of people standing around the dispatcher. An argument was evidently in progress.

"That fat dame," said England, "is Mrs. Blant. She's going to see her daughter's wedding. She better put a waddle on or she'll miss the bells."

"Gee, do you know all of them?"

"There's a fellow there in brown I don't know," said England. "But the rest of them . . . That guy in the blue overcoat is sealing a construction job this afternoon and he's just about got time to make it. That young gentleman is Secretary Lansing's boy, on his way back—"

"Here comes a girl and an old dame," said Duffy. "Know them?"

Pete England leaned forward and looked across Duffy's uniformed chest. He scowled and shook his head.

"Nope," said England, "and what's more, we haven't got room for them. Boy, that old gal sure would break a mirror."

"The girl ain't so bad. Look there, Mister England! If that isn't sable she's wearing, I'll eat it hair by hair."

"Probably rabbit," said Pete. "What the hell is Dan up to?"

The dispatcher was following the pair out to the ship. Above the mutter of the props, the pilots could hear the angry protest of the regular passengers.

"Now what in the name of the devil is this all about?" scowled England.

The dispatcher thrust his face through the door and balanced upon a wheel. "All right, Pete. On your way."

"All right hell," said Pete. "You sending me north empty?"

"You've got two," said the dispatcher.

"But what about Mrs. Blant?" said Pete. "Her gal's getting married this—"

"Never mind," said the dispatcher. "Number Six will hit here in about thirty minutes. We'll send Johnson right back with this bunch."

"You mean," said Pete, ominously, "that you'll gow up the whole day's schedule and maybe leave me overnight in New York just to send this dame and her grandma north? You're dizzy as a cuckoo clock, Dan."

"Never mind how dizzy I am. On your horse, Pete."

"She must be awful damned important," said Pete.

"She paid double for every seat in the ship. She's plenty important. Take it easy, Pete."

Savagely, England gunned the four throttles. The big kite rushed away from the awning, braked in a half circle, charged toward the end of the runway, whipped into the wind and stopped.

Out of habit, Pete swept his glance over the panel.

"Wait a minute," said Duffy.

"What the hell—"

A hand fell on Pete's shoulder. He turned and looked back into the cabin. Right behind him and looming over him stood the old lady. Her face was proud and haughty. She had the appearance of a battle-scarred general commanding troops in a charge. Her beady eyes drilled twin holes in England.

"I beg your pardon, sir," said the old lady, "but I must be quite certain that you are competent to fly this machine."

Pete gulped. He turned red. A blast of hurricane intensity almost left his lips. He swallowed it, choked on it and then managed, "Quite competent, I am sure, madam."

"I must see your pilot's license, sir."

Pete swallowed again. He dug angrily into his pocket and yanked out a compact folder stamped "Master Airline Pilot, D of C."

The old lady took it and carried it back to the girl.

Pete's view of the young lady was obscured by her companion's back, but he did see that the coat was really sable even at that distance. She was, he grudgingly muttered, a looker, damn her.

The old lady came back and handed Pete his license. "Her Highness is quite satisfied, sir. You may proceed."

Pete blinked at the title, but for a second only.

The old lady added in a wintery tone, "You will, of course, fly low and slow, sir. And please avoid the bumps."

"Yes, ma'am," gritted Pete.

The four throttles leaped ahead under his savage hand. The kite lashed down the runway, bit air, came off as lightly as a puff of smoke, streaked around to the north, climbing, and leveled out for New York.

"She said 'Her Highness,'" said the awed Duffy. "Gee, Mister England, you don't suppose she's royalty or something, do you?"

"I'd like to crown her with a crankshaft," vowed Pete.

To find out more about *The Battling Pilot* and how you can obtain your copy, go to www.goldenagestories.com.

Glossary

STORIES FROM THE GOLDEN AGE *reflect the words and expressions used in the 1930s and 1940s, adding unique flavor and authenticity to the tales. While a character's speech may often reflect regional origins, it also can convey attitudes common in the day. So that readers can better grasp such cultural and historical terms, uncommon words or expressions of the era, the following glossary has been provided.*

Albany night boat: one of a large number of river steamers formerly common to the Hudson River and patronized by New York City residents, vacationers and newlyweds.

amphibian: an airplane designed for taking off from and landing on both land and water.

Amur: Amur River, the world's ninth longest river that forms the border between northeastern China (Manchuria) and the Russian Far East (between Siberia and the Pacific Ocean). It was an area of conflict during the war between China and Japan that began in 1937, and eventually led to World War II in the Pacific.

astern: in a position behind a specified vessel.

ballyhoo: to advertise or publicize noisily or blatantly.

Black Hills: a small isolated mountain range in western South Dakota and extending into Wyoming. The Black Hills are home to the tallest peaks in continental North America east of the Rocky Mountains.

bull: a gross blunder.

bumboat: a boat used in peddling provisions and small wares among vessels lying in port or offshore.

bung starter: a wooden mallet used for tapping on the bung (cork or stopper) to loosen it from a barrel.

cabin job: an airplane that has an enclosed section where passengers can sit or cargo is stored.

castellated clouds: cloud formation named for its tower-like projections that billow upwards from the base of the cloud.

China Clipper: one of three Martin M-130 flying boats designed and built by the Glenn L. Martin Company for Pan American Airways in the 1930s. The planes, called Clippers and named for the swift square-rigged sailing ships of the 1800s, were designed to take off and land on water and possessed long-range flying capabilities. The China Clipper started flying passengers in 1936 from San Francisco to Manila making the 8,050 mile (13,683 km) trip in 60 hours of actual flying time spanning five days with stopovers in Hawaii, Midway Island, Wake Island, Guam and Manila.

Coeur d'Alene: city located in northern Idaho, on the northern shore of the Coeur d'Alene Lake and the western edge of the Coeur d'Alene National Forest. The city is named for the Coeur d'Alene tribe of Native Americans, a name given them by the French traders meaning "heart of awl," or "sharp-hearted" out of respect for their trading practices.

crown fire: a fire that *crowns* (spreads to the top branches of trees) and can spread at an incredible pace through the top of a forest. Crown fires can be extremely dangerous to all inhabitants underneath, as they may spread faster than they can be outrun, particularly on windy days.

davits: any of various cranelike devices, used singly or in pairs, for supporting, raising and lowering boats, anchors and cargo over a hatchway or side of a ship.

DeVry: manufacturer of 35mm and 16mm movie cameras popular in the 1930s, especially with newsreel cameramen.

flying boat: a seaplane whose main body is a hull adapted for floating.

foredeck: the forward part of a boat's main deck.

Frisco: San Francisco.

gig: a boat reserved for the use of the captain of a ship.

G-men: government men; agents of the Federal Bureau of Investigation.

gow up: to make sticky or mess something up. From *gow*, meaning opium or sap; the sticky brown resin harvested from poppies. Used figuratively.

gumbo: soil that turns very sticky and muddy when it becomes wet; found throughout the central US.

gunwale: the upper edge of the side of a boat. Originally a gunwale was a platform where guns were mounted, and was designed to accommodate the additional stresses imposed by the artillery being used.

Han River: a river, about 700 miles long (1,126 km), of east central China flowing generally southeast to the Yangtze River.

Jonah: one who is believed to bring bad luck or misfortune; also called a jinx. The name originated from the Old Testament prophet, *Jonah*, who by disobeying God's command caused a storm to endanger the ship he was traveling in.

kite: an airplane.

lampblack: a black pigment made from soot.

Lord Chesterfield: English politician and writer best known for *Letters to His Son* (1774), which portrays the ideal eighteenth-century gentleman.

man-o'-war: any armed ship of a national navy, usually carrying between 20 and 120 guns.

Medusa: (Greek mythology) monster with live venomous snakes for hair; people who looked at her would turn to stone. A hero, Perseus, was able to kill Medusa, aiming his sword by looking at her reflection in a highly polished shield, and then cutting off her head.

Nakajima: the name for the aircraft produced by the Nakajima Aircraft Company, Japan's first aircraft manufacturer, founded in 1917.

newshawk: a newspaper reporter, especially one who is energetic and aggressive.

painter: a rope, usually at the bow, for fastening a boat to a ship, stake, etc.

Perseus: (Greek mythology) hero who killed Medusa. The god Hermes and goddess Athena helped him in this brave deed by giving him winged shoes, a magical sword and a polished shield. With the help of these, he swooped down on Medusa from the air, used the shield as a mirror, and cut off her head without looking at her directly—as anyone who looked at her turned to stone.

Rising Sun: Japan; the characters that make up Japan's name mean "the sun's origin," which is why Japan is sometimes identified as the "Land of the Rising Sun." It is also the military flag of Japan and was used as the ensign of the Imperial Japanese Navy and the war flag of the Imperial Japanese Army until the end of World War II.

Scheherazade: the female narrator of *The Arabian Nights*, who during one thousand and one adventurous nights saved her life by entertaining her husband, the king, with stories.

sculling oar: a single oar that is moved from side to side at the stern of a boat to propel it forward.

siege guns: heavy guns for siege operations, used to overcome the target with bombardment. (A *siege* is a military operation in which an army surrounds a fortified place and isolates it while continuing to attack.)

slipped: caused (a descending parachute) to glide in a particular direction by pulling down on suspension lines on the side toward the desired direction so as to spill air out of the opposite side of the canopy.

slipstream: the airstream pushed back by a revolving aircraft propeller.

smeared: smashed.

snap-brim: a felt hat with a dented crown, and the brim turned up in back and down in front.

SS: steamship.

stall: a situation in which an aircraft suddenly dives because the airflow is obstructed and lift is lost. The loss of airflow can be caused by insufficient airspeed or by an excessive angle of an airfoil (part of an aircraft's surface that provides lift or control) when the aircraft is climbing.

struts: supports for a structure such as an aircraft wing, roof or bridge.

tarmac: airport runway.

tracer: a bullet or shell whose course is made visible by a trail of flames or smoke, used to assist in aiming.

volplaning: gliding toward the earth in an airplane, with no motor power or with the power shut off.

L. Ron Hubbard
in the Golden Age
of Pulp Fiction

In writing an adventure story
a writer has to know that he is adventuring
for a lot of people who cannot.
The writer has to take them here and there
about the globe and show them
excitement and love and realism.
As long as that writer is living the part of an
adventurer when he is hammering
the keys, he is succeeding with his story.

Adventuring is a state of mind.
If you adventure through life, you have a
good chance to be a success on paper.

Adventure doesn't mean globe-trotting,
exactly, and it doesn't mean great deeds.
Adventuring is like art.
You have to live it to make it real.

— *L. Ron Hubbard*

L. Ron Hubbard
and American
Pulp Fiction

BORN March 13, 1911, L. Ron Hubbard lived a life at least as expansive as the stories with which he enthralled a hundred million readers through a fifty-year career.

Originally hailing from Tilden, Nebraska, he spent his formative years in a classically rugged Montana, replete with the cowpunchers, lawmen and desperadoes who would later people his Wild West adventures. And lest anyone imagine those adventures were drawn from vicarious experience, he was not only breaking broncs at a tender age, he was also among the few whites ever admitted into Blackfoot society as a bona fide blood brother. While if only to round out an otherwise rough and tumble youth, his mother was that rarity of her time—a thoroughly educated woman—who introduced her son to the classics of Occidental literature even before his seventh birthday.

But as any dedicated L. Ron Hubbard reader will attest, his world extended far beyond Montana. In point of fact, and as the son of a United States naval officer, by the age of eighteen he had traveled over a quarter of a million miles. Included therein were three Pacific crossings to a then still mysterious Asia, where he ran with the likes of Her British Majesty's agent-in-place

L. Ron Hubbard, left, at Congressional Airport, Washington, DC, 1931, with members of George Washington University flying club.

for North China, and the last in the line of Royal Magicians from the court of Kublai Khan. For the record, L. Ron Hubbard was also among the first Westerners to gain admittance to forbidden Tibetan monasteries below Manchuria, and his photographs of China's Great Wall long graced American geography texts.

Upon his return to the United States and a hasty completion of his interrupted high school education, the young Ron Hubbard entered George Washington University. There, as fans of his aerial adventures may have heard, he earned his wings as a pioneering barnstormer at the dawn of American aviation. He also earned a place in free-flight record books for the longest sustained flight above Chicago. Moreover, as a roving reporter for *Sportsman Pilot* (featuring his first professionally penned articles), he further helped inspire a generation of pilots who would take America to world airpower.

Immediately beyond his sophomore year, Ron embarked on the first of his famed ethnological expeditions, initially to then untrammeled Caribbean shores (descriptions of which would later fill a whole series of West Indies mystery-thrillers). That the Puerto Rican interior would also figure into the future of Ron Hubbard stories was likewise no accident. For in addition to cultural studies of the island, a 1932–33

LRH expedition is rightly remembered as conducting the first complete mineralogical survey of a Puerto Rico under United States jurisdiction.

There was many another adventure along this vein: As a lifetime member of the famed Explorers Club, L. Ron Hubbard charted North Pacific waters with the first shipboard radio direction finder, and so pioneered a long-range navigation system universally employed until the late twentieth century. While not to put too fine an edge on it, he also held a rare Master Mariner's license to pilot any vessel, of any tonnage in any ocean.

Yet lest we stray too far afield, there is an LRH note at this juncture in his saga, and it reads in part:

"I started out writing for the pulps, writing the best I knew, writing for every mag on the stands, slanting as well as I could."

Capt. L. Ron Hubbard in Ketchikan, Alaska, 1940, on his Alaskan Radio Experimental Expedition, the first of three voyages conducted under the Explorers Club flag.

To which one might add: His earliest submissions date from the summer of 1934, and included tales drawn from true-to-life Asian adventures, with characters roughly modeled on British/American intelligence operatives he had known in Shanghai. His early Westerns were similarly peppered with details drawn from personal experience. Although therein lay a first hard lesson from the often cruel world of the pulps. His first Westerns were soundly rejected as lacking the authenticity of a Max Brand yarn (a particularly frustrating comment given L. Ron Hubbard's Westerns came straight from his Montana homeland, while Max Brand was a mediocre New York poet named Frederick Schiller Faust, who turned out implausible six-shooter tales from the terrace of an Italian villa).

Nevertheless, and needless to say, L. Ron Hubbard persevered and soon earned a reputation as among the most publishable names in pulp fiction, with a ninety percent placement rate of first-draft manuscripts. He was also among the most prolific, averaging between seventy and a hundred thousand words a month. Hence the rumors that L. Ron Hubbard had redesigned a typewriter for faster keyboard action and pounded out manuscripts on a continuous roll of butcher paper to save the precious seconds it took to insert a single sheet of paper into manual typewriters of the day.

That all L. Ron Hubbard stories did not run beneath said byline is yet another aspect of pulp fiction lore. That is, as publishers periodically rejected manuscripts from top-drawer authors if only to avoid paying top dollar, L. Ron Hubbard and company just as frequently replied with submissions under various pseudonyms. In Ron's case, the

---

A MAN OF MANY NAMES

Between 1934 and 1950, L. Ron Hubbard authored more than fifteen million words of fiction in more than two hundred classic publications. To supply his fans and editors with stories across an array of genres and pulp titles, he adopted fifteen pseudonyms in addition to his already renowned L. Ron Hubbard byline.

Winchester Remington Colt
Lt. Jonathan Daly
Capt. Charles Gordon
Capt. L. Ron Hubbard
Bernard Hubbel
Michael Keith
Rene Lafayette
Legionnaire 148
Legionnaire 14830
Ken Martin
Scott Morgan
Lt. Scott Morgan
Kurt von Rachen
Barry Randolph
Capt. Humbert Reynolds

---

list included: Rene Lafayette, Captain Charles Gordon, Lt. Scott Morgan and the notorious Kurt von Rachen—supposedly on the lam for a murder rap, while hammering out two-fisted prose in Argentina. The point: While L. Ron Hubbard as Ken Martin spun stories of Southeast Asian intrigue, LRH as Barry Randolph authored tales of

L. Ron Hubbard, circa 1930, at the outset of a literary career that would finally span half a century.

romance on the Western range—which, stretching between a dozen genres is how he came to stand among the two hundred elite authors providing close to a million tales through the glory days of American Pulp Fiction.

In evidence of exactly that, by 1936 L. Ron Hubbard was literally leading pulp fiction's elite as president of New York's American Fiction Guild. Members included a veritable pulp hall of fame: Lester "Doc Savage" Dent, Walter "The Shadow" Gibson, and the legendary Dashiell Hammett—to cite but a few.

Also in evidence of just where L. Ron Hubbard stood within his first two years on the American pulp circuit: By the spring of 1937, he was ensconced in Hollywood, adopting a Caribbean thriller for Columbia Pictures, remembered today as *The Secret of Treasure Island*. Comprising fifteen thirty-minute episodes, the L. Ron Hubbard screenplay led to the most profitable matinée serial in Hollywood history. In accord with Hollywood culture, he was thereafter continually called upon

The 1937 Secret of Treasure Island, *a fifteen-episode serial adapted for the screen by L. Ron Hubbard from his novel,* Murder at Pirate Castle.

to rewrite/doctor scripts—most famously for long-time friend and fellow adventurer Clark Gable.

In the interim—and herein lies another distinctive chapter of the L. Ron Hubbard story—he continually worked to open Pulp Kingdom gates to up-and-coming authors. Or, for that matter, anyone who wished to write. It was a fairly unconventional stance, as markets were already thin and competition razor sharp. But the fact remains, it was an L. Ron Hubbard hallmark that he vehemently lobbied on behalf of young authors—regularly supplying instructional articles to trade journals, guest-lecturing to short story classes at George Washington University and Harvard, and even founding his own creative writing competition. It was established in 1940, dubbed the Golden Pen, and guaranteed winners both New York representation and publication in *Argosy*.

But it was John W. Campbell Jr.'s *Astounding Science Fiction* that finally proved the most memorable LRH vehicle. While every fan of L. Ron Hubbard's galactic epics undoubtedly knows the story, it nonetheless bears repeating: By late 1938, the pulp publishing magnate of Street & Smith was determined to revamp *Astounding Science Fiction* for broader readership. In particular, senior editorial director F. Orlin Tremaine called for stories with a stronger *human element*. When acting editor John W. Campbell balked, preferring his spaceship-driven tales, Tremaine enlisted Hubbard. Hubbard, in turn, replied with the genre's first truly *character-driven* works, wherein heroes are pitted not against bug-eyed monsters but the mystery and majesty of deep space itself—and thus was launched the Golden Age of Science Fiction.

The names alone are enough to quicken the pulse of any science fiction aficionado, including LRH friend and protégé, Robert Heinlein, Isaac Asimov, A. E. van Vogt and Ray Bradbury. Moreover, when coupled with LRH stories of fantasy, we further come to what's rightly been described as the

foundation of every modern tale of horror: L. Ron Hubbard's immortal *Fear.* It was rightly proclaimed by Stephen King as one of the very few works to genuinely warrant that overworked term "classic"—as in: *"This is a classic tale of creeping, surreal menace and horror. . . . This is one of the really, really good ones."*

To accommodate the greater body of L. Ron Hubbard fantasies, Street & Smith inaugurated *Unknown*—a classic pulp if there ever was one, and wherein readers were soon thrilling to the likes of *Typewriter in the Sky* and *Slaves of Sleep* of which Frederik Pohl would declare: *"There are bits and pieces from Ron's work that became part of the language in ways that very few other writers managed."*

L. Ron Hubbard, 1948, among fellow science fiction luminaries at the World Science Fiction Convention in Toronto.

And, indeed, at J. W. Campbell Jr.'s insistence, Ron was regularly drawing on themes from the Arabian Nights and so introducing readers to a world of genies, jinn, Aladdin and Sinbad—all of which, of course, continue to float through cultural mythology to this day.

At least as influential in terms of post-apocalypse stories was L. Ron Hubbard's 1940 *Final Blackout*. Generally acclaimed as the finest anti-war novel of the decade and among the ten best works of the genre ever authored—here, too, was a tale that would live on in ways few other writers imagined.

Hence, the later Robert Heinlein verdict: "Final Blackout *is as perfect a piece of science fiction as has ever been written.*"

Like many another who both lived and wrote American pulp adventure, the war proved a tragic end to Ron's sojourn in the pulps. He served with distinction in four theaters and was highly decorated for commanding corvettes in the North Pacific. He was also grievously wounded in combat, lost many a close friend and colleague and thus resolved to say farewell to pulp fiction and devote himself to what it had supported these many years—namely, his serious research.

Portland, Oregon, 1943; L. Ron Hubbard, captain of the US Navy subchaser PC 815.

But in no way was the LRH literary saga at an end, for as he wrote some thirty years later, in 1980:

"Recently there came a period when I had little to do. This was novel in a life so crammed with busy years, and I decided to amuse myself by writing a novel that was pure *science fiction."*

That work was *Battlefield Earth: A Saga of the Year 3000*. It was an immediate *New York Times* bestseller and, in fact, the first international science fiction blockbuster in decades. It was not, however, L. Ron Hubbard's magnum opus, as that distinction is generally reserved for his next and final work: The 1.2 million word *Mission Earth*.

> **Final Blackout**
> *is as perfect a piece of science fiction as has ever been written.*
>
> —Robert Heinlein

How he managed those 1.2 million words in just over twelve months is yet another piece of the L. Ron Hubbard legend. But the fact remains, he did indeed author a ten-volume *dekalogy* that lives in publishing history for the fact that each and every volume of the series was also a *New York Times* bestseller.

Moreover, as subsequent generations discovered L. Ron Hubbard through republished works and novelizations of his screenplays, the mere fact of his name on a cover signaled an international bestseller. . . . Until, to date, sales of his works exceed hundreds of millions, and he otherwise remains among the most enduring and widely read authors in literary history. Although as a final word on the tales of L. Ron Hubbard, perhaps it's enough to simply reiterate what editors told readers in the glory days of American Pulp Fiction:

He writes the way he does, brothers, because he's been there, seen it and done it!

THE STORIES FROM THE
GOLDEN AGE

Your ticket to adventure starts here with the Stories from
the Golden Age collection by master storyteller L. Ron Hubbard.
These gripping tales are set in a kaleidoscope of exotic locales and brim
with fascinating characters, including some of the
most vile villains, dangerous dames and brazen heroes
you'll ever get to meet.

The entire collection of over one hundred and fifty stories is being
released in a series of eighty books and audiobooks.
For an up-to-date listing of available titles,
go to www.goldenagestories.com.

AIR ADVENTURE

FAR-FLUNG ADVENTURE

SEA ADVENTURE

TALES FROM THE ORIENT

MYSTERY

FANTASY

Borrowed Glory   *If I Were You*
The Crossroads   *The Last Drop*
Danger in the Dark   *The Room*
The Devil's Rescue   *The Tramp*
He Didn't Like Cats

SCIENCE FICTION

The Automagic Horse   *A Matter of Matter*
Battle of Wizards   *The Obsolete Weapon*
Battling Bolto   *One Was Stubborn*
The Beast   *The Planet Makers*
Beyond All Weapons   *The Professor Was a Thief*
A Can of Vacuum   *The Slaver*
The Conroy Diary   *Space Can*
The Dangerous Dimension   *Strain*
Final Enemy   *Tough Old Man*
The Great Secret   *240,000 Miles Straight Up*
Greed   *When Shadows Fall*
The Invaders

128

WESTERN

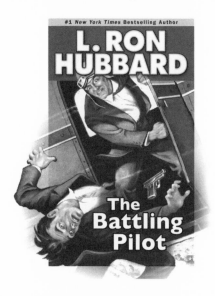

JOIN THE PULP REVIVAL
America in the 1930s and 40s

Pulp fiction was in its heyday and 30 million readers were regularly riveted by the larger-than-life tales of master storyteller L. Ron Hubbard. For this was pulp fiction's golden age, when the writing was raw and every page packed a walloping punch.

That magic can now be yours. An evocative world of nefarious villains, exotic intrigues, courageous heroes and heroines—a world that today's cinema has barely tapped for tales of adventure and swashbucklers.

Enroll today in the Stories from the Golden Age Club and begin receiving your monthly feature edition selected from more than 150 stories in the collection.

You may choose to enjoy them as either a paperback or audiobook for the special membership price of $9.95 each month along with FREE shipping and handling.

CALL TOLL-FREE: **1-877-8GALAXY**
(1-877-842-5299) OR GO ONLINE TO
www.goldenagestories.com
AND BECOME PART OF THE PULP REVIVAL!

Prices are set in US dollars only. For non-US residents, please call
1-323-466-7815 for pricing information. Free shipping available for US residents only.

Galaxy Press, 7051 Hollywood Blvd., Suite 200, Hollywood, CA 90028